ABSOLUTE UNIT

OR:
THE BOREDOM OF THE STALINGRAD SNIPER

NICK KOLAKOWSKI

Let the world know:
#IGotMyCLPBook!

Crystal Lake Publishing
www.CrystalLakePub.com

OTHER NOVELLA RECOMMENDATIONS:

Of Men and Monsters by Tom Deady
Eight Cylinders by Jason Parent
Hollow Heart by Ben Eads
The Pale White by Chad Lutzke
Little Dead Red by Mercedes M. Yardley
The Final Reconciliation by Todd Keisling
Run to Ground by Jasper Bark
Wind Chill by Patrick Rutigliano

WELCOME
TO ANOTHER

CRYSTAL LAKE PUBLISHING
CREATION

Join today at www.crystallakepub.com & www.patreon.com/CLP

WELCOME TO ANOTHER CRYSTAL LAKE PUBLISHING CREATION.

Thank you for supporting independent publishing and small presses. You rock, and hopefully you'll quickly realize why we've become one of the world's leading publishers of Dark Fiction and Horror. We have some of the world's best fans for a reason, and hopefully we'll be able to add you to that list really soon.

To follow us behind the scenes (while supporting independent publishing and our authors), be sure to join our interactive community of authors and readers on Patreon (https://www.patreon.com/CLP) for exclusive content. You can even subscribe to all our future releases. Otherwise drop by our website and online store (www.crystallakepub.com/). We'd love to have you.

Welcome to Crystal Lake Publishing—Tales from the Darkest Depths.

1.

EVERY DAY, ALL DAY, Bill smells shit or burning hair. Bill asks everybody if they smell those things, and when they say no ("What smell, dude?"), Bill thinks they're lying to him. (Bill, your friendly neighborhood health inspector, thinks everybody lies to him.) Only when Bill starts smelling the distinct odor of his wife's crotch does he begin to suspect something's well and truly wrong with the ol' noggin— she's been dead for years.

Not that Bill will see a doctor about his symptoms, no sir. Instead he'll smoke and snort and screw the fear away, because a buzz always beats reality, and the idea of a tumor or an artery primed to blow is as real as it gets. On Monday, Bill takes two hundred dollars in hankie-soft bills from a corner market, in exchange for overlooking a frisky roach, and uses it to purchase a few small bags of the finest chemical concoction some creep could cook up in a kitchen sink, which he smokes in the front seat of his Official Government Vehicle before driving to his favorite strip club. That fine institution always earns an 'A' when inspection time rolls around, in exchange for a regular gratis lunch of a burger and pints and a bored lap-dance from someone who'd rather be anywhere but near him.

We sense the disgusted look on your face. Really, what else do you expect poor Bill to do? Born with a nubby penis and a tendency toward obesity, the meat computer in his skull loaded with buggy software, it's a miracle that Bill made it this far. A thousand years ago, he would have been a sex toy for Vikings on his way to becoming worm food. These days, the twin wonders of medical technology and modern law will ensure that he lives long enough to realize he can't obliterate the memories of his dead wife and all his failures, no matter how hard he tries.

But we're going to help him, mostly because we don't have a choice. Bill is our home.

2.

E WERE BORN on a Greek cargo ship bound for the East Coast. Like many an immigrant before us, our childhood was messy and short. The sailors pushed the lever that dumped the bilge tanks, and we found ourselves floating off the scenic coast of New Jersey, where the current soon directed us to an inlet, and from there to a pipe, and soon enough we sloshed through the speedy water-park of the local waste-treatment plant, where we slipped through a corroded filter on our way to Bill's kitchen tap, and from there to Bill's glass, and from there to Bill's stomach, which offered everything an enthusiastic young parasite could ever desire: water, proteins, microbes on which to snack, and drugs—beautiful, weird drugs.

Fortunately for us, Bill can't even endure the twenty-minute drive from strip club to office without snorting a small pile of crushed-up pills. Got to balance out those five pints of cheap beer *somehow*. Forehead red and sweaty, heart hammering, pupils squeezed to pinpricks, Bill can barely see the road; so how, might you ask, can we see through his eyes? Like the vine that wraps the tree, we have tendrils everywhere, from his balls to his brain, where we've tapped into the sparking neurons that convey visuals and sound.

Bill makes it back to the office after two near-accidents, pausing outside the parking garage to smoke another cigarette and check his appearance in a window, nodding in approval at his bloodshot eyes and trembling fingers and tragic hair. Maybe he doesn't let himself see the fractures; maybe he thinks they're normal; or maybe (and this is the worst option) Bill has chosen to embrace his sorry-ass state. It's hard for us to tell because, despite our bits woven deep into his core, we can't yet read his thoughts, although we have big hopes for the pink thread we've extended to the base of his skull, poised to wrap around his brainstem like a lasso.

Bill's office is a windowless hive of gray cubicles stretching to infinity, lit only by fluorescents that make everyone look like a corpse. He enters the office like a returning conqueror, arms thrown wide, emitting a wordless scream of mock bloodlust, only for his little routine to run smack into what we like to call the Unbreakable Wall of Despair, a.k.a. his coworkers. They glance from their spreadsheets and email long enough to confirm Bill's utter lack of threat, then return to their screens without a word.

A new and as-yet-unlit cigarette pasted in the corner of his lips, Bill helps himself to a mug of primordial brew from the coffee pot and saunters over to Janine, his flame in Accounts Receivable. Janine is a rare specimen in these parts, still holding some hope that one day she'll escape this place with health and sanity intact. She's still so young, at least two or three Bills away from overcoming this desire to save broken men with her love. The Fear is starting to settle in her, though—we don't need a tendril in her brain to know she worries that she's too heavy, too dumb, too unlucky to fulfill her puniest hopes. We want to tell her it's okay, that anyone can climb the ladder of the American Dream. If a parasite from a freighter bilge can hitch a ride aboard a government worker with a decent ticker and a major substance-abuse problem, a *homo sapien* with her skills can score a split-level with okay water pressure outside of Trenton.

But we can't speak through Bill, who looks around to see if anybody's watching before reaching down to cup her soft ass. She slaps his arm, playfully, and flicks her eyes toward the nearby stairwell, which leads to a little-used storage room where three times a week we spend no more than four minutes staring at the moist, pale expanse of her back as she braces against Bill's mushy hip-thrusts (minutes we dearly wish to erase from memory, we hasten to add). Oh, Janine, you can do so much better.

Janine and Bill, they're bonded like ticks and dogs. When Bill's older brother died a couple months ago, Janine outdid herself at the funeral, unleashing a glass-shattering wail just as Bill dropped the first shovel of dirt on the coffin. Her grief warmed Bill's heart, articulated all the things he refused to let himself feel. Bill's brother may have raised him, but by the end Bill didn't have the cojones to come to the hospital and say goodbye. Sometimes we think it's not quite enough to save Bill's body: we have to save his soul, as well.

In the dimness of the storage room Bill pumps frantically away at Janine, sweating, heart thundering so hard it makes us more than a little concerned about a coronary in the near future. The alcohol from lunch must have dulled the nerves in his Midnight Meat Train, because it takes a full five minutes longer than usual for him to finish up . . . and when he does, we bask in that endorphin bliss, marveling at how it makes his shambles of a nervous system light up like Times Square on New Year's Eve. Such glories are invisible to Bill, who fumbles his substandard package back into his pants and, with a wheeze and a muttered term of endearment, shuffles back downstairs.

3.

A FEW DAYS LATER—and three hours late, but who's counting—Bill's crumpled soda-can of a jalopy (his personal car, mind you, not that government-funded monster) murmurs its way into the lone empty parking space of a coffee shop near his house, the engine cutting out with a loud fart, Bill emerging in full Sunday-morning glory. From his leather jacket, dry and cracked as the surface of Mars, he extracts a crumpled cigarette and torches up, exhaling a cloud of fragrant smoke. In that moment, taking a fresh jolt of poison into his bruised lungs, he seems almost human again: his spine straightens, his cheeks flush from bloodless pale to heart-attack red (an improvement, trust us), his cloudy gaze clears into the speculative laser-stare of Ye Olden Days, when Bill could still put on a good show of walking the earth larger than life.

Bill power-draws the cigarette in four long pulls, crushes the leftover bit beneath his scuffed heel before heading inside, where his nephew Trent—a hot mess, that one—jitters over his seventh cup of coffee and the last crumbs of a chocolate-chip muffin. The coffee shop is an old-school joint, all chipped Formica and torn vinyl benches, the radio playing Frank Sinatra instead of whatever electronica Trent no doubt prefers.

Bill takes a seat, offering Trent a close-up view of his wreckage, the bloodshot eyes and flaking lips and graying hairs corkscrewing from his chin. Bill had a bad week: two Chinese restaurants refused to pay his little toll (the nerve) and his Friday jaunt with Janine ended with a bad case of whiskey-dick. When the waitress arrives, he orders a cup of coffee and a doughnut.

"Rough night?" Trent says.

Kid, if you had any idea of what we face on a daily basis. Every time Bill puffs down too many cigarettes, or pops a pill of questionable origin, or decides to drown his sorrows in a tide of flavored vodka, we feel it in the same way that a sailor, clinging to the railing of a freighter during a fierce storm, endures the next monster wave crashing over him. Once upon a time it was fun to take that ride, but those days are fading in our metaphorical rearview mirror. We would hurl, if our parasitic form came with a stomach. We would beg for mercy, if we could actually use Bill's mouth.

Bill leans back, scanning Trent's liberal use of eyeliner, the leopard-print jacket with the white fuzzy collar, the strands of fake pearls around the kid's thin neck.

"What's that I smell?" he rasps, after taking a loud sniff. "Perfume?"

"Cologne. Trying to be presentable, you know."

"More like trying to get beat." Bill makes a great show of shrugging. "Anyway, what you need, kid?"

"Your brother—"

"Your father, you mean. Show some respect."

"He didn't leave me any money."

"That's why you call me, at eight on a Sunday?"

Trent turns checking his watch into a piece of theater. The dramatics run deep in this family: every slight, every comeback elevated to the level of Shakespeare. "Yeah, and it's almost ten when you show up."

"I know what time it is," Bill says. "You're nearly seventeen, Trent. You can handle yourself, right? You can get along in the world."

Trent opens his mouth to respond when the waitress comes around, bearing a fresh pot of coffee and Bill's doughnut. She fills their coffee cups, and Bill reaches out, very delicately, to pinch her sleeve—holding her in place as he downs the cup in one swallow, places it back on the saucer, and cocks an eyebrow for a refill. The waitress raises the coffee pot, as if to dump it in his lap, but fulfills the request. Everybody pities stray dogs.

"Anyway," Bill says, after draining his second cup. "I got work all day. Don't you got a friend you can call? That cute girl you used to hang out with?"

"Nobody's picking up." Trent's breath hitches a little, and we can hear the boy trying hard not to let his voice waver. "They're all sick of me."

"Nonsense, they're probably still asleep." Bill crams his breakfast down his throat, gifting us with a bright sugar rush. "You need cash? I got cash."

"I got ten bucks, which should get me through today. No, I want you to take me with you."

"Where?"

"To work. Show me what you do. How you earn."

"You know what I do. Besides, it's Sunday. We don't usually do inspections on Sunday."

"I'm not talking about inspections. I'm talking about . . . you know . . . the shakedown."

"This conversation's over." Bill half-stands.

"Not if I tell someone at your office, it isn't."

Bill thumps down. "Come on, kid. Give me a break."

"Trust me, I'll find it fascinating. Seeing how the world really works."

Bill rolls his eyes. "You don't know anything."

"Besides, I want to hang out with you. I never see you." Trent picks up his chocolate-smeared knife and runs a thumb along the blade. "Show me. Or I'll tell."

"Okay." He's a pushover, our Bill. He likes to think he's a tough guy. If you pour a couple drinks in him, he'll even try to act the part. But Bill knows he's a bottom-feeder, and all bottom-feeders like company. Trust us on that one.

4.

BILL HAS THE guts to show the kid an actual workday. They hustle a diner over on Bedford ("Is that mouse poop I see?"), raking in a princely ninety bucks, before pulling into the gravel lot behind Paradise Alley at a quarter past eleven. Bill shows the faintest modicum of decency by ordering his nephew to stay in the car while he goes inside Paradise Alley "for a minute." Poor kid, hopefully he'll prove smart enough to crack a window within the next hour, lest he fry in the late-morning heat like a puppy.

Bill really means to have a shot of whiskey or two, the early lunch of champions, but he finds his best friend Frank at the bar, loading up. Frank is a homicide dick (emphasis on the word "dick") who lives with his mother, snorts mountains of coke swiped from the evidence locker, and recites more Bible verses than a street preacher. He's such a walking contradiction it's a wonder that he can stride more than a block without vaporizing into thin air, his warring impulses canceling him out of existence like a negative subtracted from a negative. Maybe someday he *will* disappear. In Bill's highly suspect vision, Frank often shimmers a bit, like a figure viewed across a wide stretch of desert.

Frank deserves a parasite with his best interests at heart, but instead he needs to make do with the voices in his head. These bottom-feeders, how do they find one another? Bill and Frank spend twenty minutes trading shots at the bar and making fun of the furnishings, which is easy to do in a place like Paradise Alley, with its cheesy neon signage and ratty moose's head over the bar. Bill is about to say adios and head back to the car when Frank claps him on the shoulder and asks for a favor.

Bill follows Frank to the far edge of the bar's parking lot, where Frank has parked his bright purple Cadillac (purchased for cheap at a police auction; he never bothered to fix the two bullet-holes in the dashboard). Frank opens the trunk to reveal an ominous-looking bundle wrapped in white sheets and bound in duct tape. Definitely a body.

His panic spiking, Bill glances at his car parked across the lot. His nephew slumps in the passenger seat, head down as he plays with his phone. When Bill looks back at Frank, the cop's cheeks are iridescent with tears.

"Can you help me, buddy?" Frank asks.

We can tell that Bill wants to ask about the identity of the body in the trunk. But if he says the wrong thing, Frank in his alcohol-powered lunacy is liable to pull his service pistol and decorate the gravel with Bill's brains. Of all the days for Bill's nephew to just show up, why the hell did it have to be this one?

Bill swallows hard and nods.

"Good. Let's take a ride." Frank tosses the keys over the roof. "You're driving."

Bill ducks into Frank's car without looking back at

his nephew, and we hope the kid will stay parked behind the bar until . . . well, whenever. Bill feels a pang of sadness (a dark tinge we can smell in his blood) at abandoning a relative. He fastens his seatbelt and takes the offered keys from Frank. The Caddy starts with a vigorous roar that vibrates everybody's gelatin in the most pleasing of ways. The crucifix dangling from the rearview mirror swings wildly as Bill slams the gas and squeals the car out of the parking lot, and Frank claps his hands in delight like an over-caffeinated child.

"You have a plan?" Bill asks, glancing up at the rearview mirror—and almost has a heart attack when he sees his jalopy in pursuit, his nephew at the wheel. Maybe the kid is brave, but knowing how this family works, that's probably wishful thinking. Trent's more likely furious, or curious, or any of those lesser devils that drive humans to do really stupid things.

"Yeah, I got a contact who owes me a favor," Frank says. "Why we're trusting something this sensitive to a bunch of trust-fund babies with hygiene issues is totally beyond my comprehension, but this is the situation and we're dealing with it."

"Huh?" Bill doesn't quite follow.

Frank cocks an eyebrow. "Eh?"

"What did I do to deserve this?" Bill says, mostly to himself.

Frank's already twisted his inner dial to a different channel. "Did I ever tell you, when I was a kid, I saw the last show Nirvana ever played? I swear, there was not a man or woman in that place who did not want to drop to their knees and suck Kurt dry right there."

"That's not a very Christian impulse, buddy."

Frank pulls his pistol and jams it into Bill's neck, spittle flying as he yells: "Show me where in the *Bible* it says that, you chunky *motherfucker.*"

Bill shakes his head, stunned into wise silence. Trapped inside his skin, we can do nothing but tighten up and hope for the best. In theory, a part of us could execute an acrobatic transfer through a bullet hole in Bill's spine, snap across the blood-humid space and down Frank's throat before the cop could so much as holler. The odds of us pulling off something like that, with bodies moving so fast, are nil. And if we think Bill's guts are terrifying, can you imagine what we would find inside Frank?

"Right," Frank says, grinding the barrel deeper. "The Bible said nothing about going down on *rock stars*, because rock stars hadn't been *invented* when Jesus walked the Earth. Can I get an Amen?"

"Amen?" Bill mutters. In the rearview mirror, his nephew continues his pursuit, wisely dropping back a few car-lengths.

"You're damn skippy." Frank tucks away the pistol and flops back in his seat, adjusting his collar with a few deft tugs. "For the love of God, Bill, why are you always so dense?"

"It's how I was raised," Bill moans.

"Indeed." Frank reaches into his pocket, extracts a bright blue pill, and swallows it dry. "That's not your kid, is it?"

Bill tries playing dumb. "What kid?"

"The one that's been following us since the bar. I'm a cop, buddy, remember?"

"Oh, that's just my nephew." Bill tries a fake chuckle. "He's a good kid. He's fine."

"He's a witness." Frank's hand strokes the pistol grip jutting out of his pants. "How close are you to him?"

"He's fine, I said. You want me to lose him?"

Frank winks. "No, let him follow. Then I'll deal with him."

Given Bill's habitual cowardice, there's every chance he'll let Frank shoot his nephew in the head. If we could finally plug that tendril into his brainstem, we could maybe take control of the ship—but we have to sort through nerves by feel, and that takes time.

Time is something we don't have in abundance. Frank gestures for Bill to take a right into an industrial wasteland, where we motor along the edge of a drainage ditch, spewing a huge cloud of dust in our wake. Trent, the idiot, accelerates until he's right behind.

Bill finally musters the courage to ask: "Who's in the trunk?" He wrinkles his nose, smelling shit, but given the environs it's hard for us to tell whether the scent is purely in his head.

"My mother," Frank says, and starts unbuttoning his shirt. "She tried to cross me on my big coke deal. You know what it's like, getting shot by the woman who gave birth to you? It doesn't just hurt physically, man." He pulls his shirt open, revealing a nasty bruise just beneath the sternum. "Good thing I always wear my bulletproof vest in the house."

"I'm sorry," Bill says, which seems like the phrase least likely to draw a lethal response from Frank, whose voice begins to shake.

"I loved her, man," Frank says, the faucets in his eyes squeaking open again. In Bill's fear-heightened state, where all sounds and sights and smells are achingly acute, we can hear a teardrop spatter Frank's shirt.

"I'm sure," Bill says.

"I loved her. I didn't mean for any of this to happen." Frank's hands tremble along with his vocal cords. He's at his weakest, distracted, his heart exposed.

We take back everything we might have said about Bill's cowardice, because we can tell he's about to do something impulsive, based on the soda-sweet tang of adrenaline flooding his bloodstream. Bill is liable to mess up whatever he's considering, but fortunately we are here to help. As his excitement peaks, we take our tendril that loops around a bundle of nerves and tendons in his calf—and pull as hard as we can. His foot slams down the gas pedal.

The Cadillac slams forward and to the left, over the edge of the ditch and airborne, just as Bill gets a hand on Frank's gun, which Frank has already pulled from his pants, gunshots bursting everybody's eardrums as the dashboard explodes. The car crunches into the far side of the ditch and Frank, without a seatbelt holding him back, tumbles through the windshield with the greatest of ease, his bones snap-crackle-popping on the way.

While Bill gasps for oxygen like a beached whale, we perform a quick damage assessment. He'll have a nasty bruise across the man-tits, and maybe a busted finger. Unlocking his seatbelt, he leans on his crumpled door until it pops open, spilling him onto the crumbling bank of the ditch. Brakes screech, followed by Trent calling out Bill's name.

Trent charges through the dust, pearls jangling, but Bill spares him the briefest look before turning to the nightmare that is Frank trying to stand on broken legs, his face glittering with broken glass embedded in his skin, his bloody hand holding the pistol.

"Why'd you do that, man?" Frank asks. He sounds offended.

"I couldn't let you hurt my family," Bill says, maybe his first ethical sentence in years, and we swear we had nothing to do with it. We would applaud, if we had hands.

"Well, you failed," Frank says, gritting his teeth in pain as he lifts the pistol. Trent spins on his heel, sprinting for the car. Bill's beyond any fancy moves at this point, but we can offer a late-game assist.

We yank the tendon again, tilting Bill into the path of the bullet. We assume a heroic sacrifice is what he wants, right? The hollow-point slug plows through his side, clipping a kidney and ruining some blood vessels, but he'll live if we can get him to a hospital in time, or if Frank doesn't shoot him between the eyes.

That second outcome looks like a definite possibility as Frank hobbles forward, babbling something incoherent about God and vengeance and cocaine. The pistol rises again, about to finish off Bill once and for all, when Bill's car bursts from the dust-cloud and plows into Frank head-on, sending everybody's favorite crooked cop through a windshield for the second time in one day. Behind the wheel, panicked Trent keeps the gas slammed down until the car rolls into the side of the crashed Cadillac, Frank's feet drumming a final solo on the hood while his mouth sputters blood all over the dashboard.

5.

RENT KNEELS BESIDE bloody Bill, his phone pressed to his ear.

"Tell . . . Janine . . . " Bill says.

"Janine who?" Trent says, after asking emergency services to haul ass down to the industrial site.

"Tell her I love her," Bill says.

Bill will have the opportunity to do so himself. Just a few more minutes and the ambulance will arrive, which will ferry Bill to a hospital, where doctors will perform all the diagnostics he so desperately needs. They'll throw him in a scanner, and hopefully pick up on whatever's making him smell the oddest things.

But wait, won't they find us, as well?

Oh crap, maybe we didn't think this one through.

Is it worth going to our possible death, knowing that we've helped Bill become a better person? Of course not. We send a tendril up Bill's throat, poised to shoot out his open mouth. If Trent would only lean a little bit closer and stay still for a second or two, we can move out of Bill for good. We'll always love our first home, but a big part of life is knowing when to say goodbye.

6.

S FAR AS hosts go, upgrading from Bill to Trent is the equivalent of going from a broken-down double-wide on the edge of a radioactive pit to a nice McMansion in a quiet subdivision. Trent's lungs are blissfully clear of ash and phlegm, his heart ticks along like a Swiss watch, and his muscles are lean and hard. Now we feel a little bad about living so long in Bill when newer models were available. But beggars can't be choosers, and when we swam out of that tanker into our new life in America, we were the textbook definition of vulnerable.

Trent has no idea we entered him. We waited until his eyes flicked left, toward the onrushing ambulance, before firing the tendril into his open mouth. He coughed, swallowed, and pounded his chest—massive booms through the cavern of his sternum as we affixed to his esophagus, then sent a sub-tendril winding through his tissues (So pink! So lovely!) toward his spine. Plugging into a convenient nerve, we could share his vision—so crisp and clear, compared to Bill's dull eyesight.

Trent stands, leaping from foot to foot as he directs the bored EMTs to focus on Bill instead of the twice-splattered Frank. Bill waves to Trent as he's loaded into the ambulance, which roars off, siren wailing. We bid a silent goodbye to the parts of us still inside our old home, which a few courses of antibiotics, plus a blast of radiation from an MRI, will surely dissolve to nothingness.

A police cruiser arrives next, vomiting out two officers: one thick and squat, his partner thin and tall. Their nametags say 'BARNES, D.' and 'GRIMES, T.' We decide to name them Tweedledum and Tweedledee, for obvious reasons. Tweedledee issues a low whistle at the sight of Frank's mangled remains, but neither seem too concerned about one of their colleagues converted into a hundred-fifty pounds of ground beef with glass chunks mixed in.

"That who I think it is?" Tweedledum asks, cocking his head for a better view.

"Abso-fucking-lutely," Tweedledee says.

"Oh man." Tweedledum chuckles. "I told Frank once, he'd crash and burn if he kept up with his bullshit, but I meant that as a metaphor, I swear."

Tweedledee turns to Trent. "What happened here?"

"Listen, believe me, okay, it was self-defense," Trent babbles. "I mean, he came at my uncle with a gun, and then a car hit him?"

"A car hit him." Tweedledee smirks at Tweedledum. "Just like that. Came out of nowhere, by itself, and smacked into poor Frank."

"That's some futuristic stuff," Tweedledum says. "Like, Elon Musk shit."

"I was driving the car, okay?" Trent clutches his hair. "I was driving it, but I didn't, like, want to kill this guy or anything, I'm not a killer, I just wanted to stop him from hurting my uncle, okay? I just wanted to stop him, because . . ."

Tweedledee wanders away, triggering the radio clipped to his chest, rattling off coordinates and codes. Trent paces faster and faster, nails digging into his skull, tears carving trails down his dusty cheeks.

"Hold up," Tweedledum raises and lowers his hands, palms down, as if that will somehow cool Trent's epic meltdown. "It's not your fault, okay? Frank was a very bad man. Had some superstar busts in his time, believe me, but he was more trouble than he was worth. Stop pacing for just one damn moment and listen to me, okay?"

Trent pauses.

"Good." Tweedledum smiles. "You're going to walk on this. Self-defense, dirty cop, what you did was totally righteous. But there's a catch, okay? You're going to leave right now, and you're going to keep silent about what happened here for the rest of your life. No press, no talk shows, nothing, got that?"

Trent tries to speak but nothing comes out.

Tweedledum's smile fades. "Because if you do speak—about any of this—it could get very bad for you, all right? Like, you might disappear one night. Nobody would hear from you again. You get me?"

Trent nods so vigorously we feel a neck-bone pop.

"Good." Tweedledum turns to regard the spectacular wreck of the purple Cadillac. Fluid drools from its cracked engine, and the frame is a crumpled mess, but the impact failed to pop the trunk with its inconvenient corpse. Just wait until the cops find that juicy treat.

"Get a move on," Tweedledum says, "before too many people show up."

"I . . ." Trent points at the wrecked cars. "Can, uh, I get a ride?"

Snorting Tweedledum points somewhere over Trent's shoulder. "There's a bus stop back that way. Saw it on the way in. I don't think you're getting your car back anytime soon."

"Yeah, those stains are never coming out," Tweedledee yells as he pokes at Frank's left foot.

Trent backs away slowly, as if expecting Tweedledum to draw his sidearm and open fire. After the events of the past hour, who could blame him? Only when Tweedledum turns away to join his partner does Trent spin around and trot for the bus stop. At the wasteland's distant edge, more police cruisers emerge from a cloud of dust, lights flashing.

All this time, we haven't been idle—although we must admit, Tweedledum's unsubtle threat makes us wonder whether our tenure in Trent might prove shorter than expected. As our new home stammered and sweated, we began weaving new connections throughout his *systema nervosum*, getting to know his neural pathways. We're a long way from accessing his thoughts, but we can sense his shame and fear in his clenched stomach, tight muscles, the way his adrenaline gland squirts in response to the faintest sound. As we guessed when we examined Trent through Bill's eyes, this is a kid who's unsure of himself, who wants someone to show him the way, to tell him that everything will be fine. Given enough time, we can become that inner voice, guiding him toward a brighter future, but we'd much prefer outright control over his body.

We hope that Trent takes good drugs on occasion,

or at least eats some very spicy meals, the cuisines that Bill tended to avoid as if a bad case of indigestion was the worst of his problems. What's the point of changing homes if you can't experience new things?

<h1 style="text-align:center">7.</h1>

T**RENT HAS A** caring heart, because after he spends half an hour ugly-crying on a park bench while listening to David Bowie on his phone, he heads to the hospital to visit his dear, injured uncle.

We've been deprived of good music. The ringing of a cash register as a harried restaurant owner slapped out a couple hundred dollars, the begging of a bodega staffer for a little more time to pay up—that was the only music for dear Bill, who always liked to play sports radio while making his rounds. If Trent spins classics cut two decades before he was born, we consider that a big step up.

Still humming "Heroes" under his breath, Trent uses his last ten dollars to buy flowers from a kiosk in the hospital lobby.

Soon enough Bill is out of surgery and bedded in the ICU, in a bright and featureless room with no art on the walls, the window-shade pulled down, the television blaring from its perch on the wall. He lies in the depths of a medically induced coma, wrapped in a cocoon of tubes and wiring, as the bedside machines beep and thump. In the hospital's antiseptic lighting he looks absolutely terrible, purple and pocked and hairy, and we suppose it's a wonder he's survived all the trauma of the day. We wonder if the bits of us in his gut are still alive, if anything managed to endure the scalpels and drugs and radiation and horrific tests. The absence of humans in biohazard suits suggests we've been overlooked in the rush to save Bill's life.

Trent hands the flowers to a nurse, who hustles away for a vase, and plops into the seat beside the bed. The television hisses that a cop has been killed. We want Trent to turn toward the screen, so we can catch the visuals, but he keeps his gaze locked on Bill.

While we wait, we send a few tendrils deeper into Trent's meat, exploring our real estate. It's all prime, the nerve bundles humming with enough electricity to power a city. We plug into one near the base of his skull, and the energy lights up our cells. From this new position, we can hear Trent thinking, although it's like hearing someone in the next room, a dull murmur, with no words we can discern. Through a tendril, we try to send a signal into his cortex, a subtle command to move his left foot.

No movement.

Well, Rome wasn't built in a day.

As we weave our way deeper, we mull over the body of Frank's mother in the Cadillac trunk. Frank shooting her over a big drug deal is a detail the cops will want to keep hidden. Or maybe they'll try to pin the whole thing on Trent. Crazy teen goes on murderous rampage, that's a hip story these days.

Trent needs to leave this hospital room as fast as possible, because sooner or later the cops will appear, but we can't move his toe, much less speak to him. Before we can formulate a solution, the door opens, and in walks a man in an off-the-rack brown suit, a gold shield clipped to his belt. His gray hair suggests middle age, but he is a square block of muscle, like he spends all his free time deadlifting cattle. He looks at Trent and says: "Mister Montague?"

"Yes?" Trent's heart thunders, sweat drenching his armpits.

"You're Bill's nephew?" The man nods toward the lump of bruised flesh on the bed.

"Yes?"

"Great." The man tries to smile, to extend warmth, but the gesture resembles a shark opening its mouth to bite. "No big deal, but you fled the scene of a crime, son. Did the officers say you could leave?"

Trent's pulse edges into heart-attack territory. "No? I mean, yes? Not really? Um . . . "

"Son." The man raises a hand. "It's okay, whatever happened. I'm here now. We can talk."

"Who . . . who are you?"

"I'm Detective Russell Mott. My partner, who'll be along in a minute, is Detective Melinda Banks. We just want to ask you a few questions about what happened out there. As you may know, we lost one of our own."

We don't need to penetrate Trent's thoughts to know he's envisioning Officers Tweedledum and Tweedledee warning him to keep his mouth shut unless he wants to end up in a ditch with most of his head missing. Trent seems like a smart lad but if he babbles the wrong thing, this situation could turn too messy for our liking. We inch a tendril into the base of his skull (Trent wincing, his hand rising toward his neck), wrap it around the correct gland, and give it a squeeze. A faint trickle of bliss-inducing dopamine hits Trent's bloodstream.

Trent's heart slows, and he takes deeper breaths. "I'm very sorry to hear that," he says. "I didn't see much. My uncle was having some kind of fight in a car? The officer was pointing a gun at him?"

Detective Mott leans against the wall beneath the television, his arms folded over his epic chest. "That 'officer' was Detective Frank Smith," he says. "He worked Homicide, and he was damn good at his job. Have you considered that maybe he was attempting to arrest your uncle?"

"Bill never killed anyone."

"Or maybe your uncle was an informant? An uncooperative one?"

"My uncle never mentioned anything like that. I don't know what to tell you."

From his inner jacket pocket, Detective Mott retrieves his phone. As he does, we catch a glimpse of his shoulder holster and its big black pistol. Tapping an app to life, he places the phone on the small table to Trent's right. "You mind if I record this?"

"Uh, yeah." Trent swallows. "Shouldn't I get a lawyer or something?"

"Why, you guilty of something? You not telling me the truth here?" Mott steps closer. "If you want a lawyer, that's your choice. I can formally arrest you, take you down to the station, shove you in a windowless room, and we can have ourselves a good, old-fashioned interrogation. You want that?"

"Um, no?"

"I didn't think so. You're not a suspect in anything." That shark-smile again. "This is just a friendly chat, because we need to know what happened to Frank. Got that?"

"Okay."

"Go."

"Like I said, they were fighting in the car, and then the officer—sorry, detective—was pointing a gun at him. Then they crashed their car into my car, and the detective came through the windshield?"

We might be a parasite, but we've watched enough cop shows through Bill's eyes to know that Trent's statement will never hold up to deeper examination. And that's before we consider the body in the trunk. When is Mott going to bring that up?

"Have you ever met Detective Smith before?" Mott asks.

Trent shakes his head.

"You sure? Your uncle never threw a party at his house, Frank happened to come around?"

"My uncle didn't really throw . . . parties."

We could take issue with that assertion: Bill often threw parties for himself, consuming enough pills and whiskey to put a fraternity house in a collective coma ("Why share?" he sometimes muttered to the ceiling. "Ungrateful assholes."). Try not to blame him: after what we've seen in the basements of some restaurants in this fair city, we'd drink to forget, too. And let's not forget his dead wife.

Trying too hard to act casual, Mott says: "He ever mention Frank's mother?"

"Um, no? I saw my uncle get pushed into the car by some guy. I followed him in case I could help. I got too close, and they crashed into me. That's everything."

"You didn't think to dial 911?"

Trent shakes his head. "I did. It said all operators busy."

"That's city infrastructure for you. Before this car chase, what were you doing?"

"I was just hanging out with my uncle, and he said we had to stop by a bar. I thought it was kind of weird, because we were having family time? Then he comes out of the bar with the detective, and, um, yeah, all that bad stuff started."

It's a sweet sentiment, Trent referring to a morning of grifting with Bill as "family time." We squeeze more dopamine into Trent's blood, enough to keep him happy but not *too* happy, and he smiles.

The door opens again, and a short woman with a buzzed-blonde scalp steps through, unsmiling. She wears jeans and a button-down blue shirt, her belt loaded down with pistol and extra clips and gold shield. "Sorry I'm late," she says, shutting the door behind her. "Had trouble parking the beast."

They exchange a look. Private joke, or a signal of some kind? Impossible to tell. The woman strides forward and crushes Trent's hand in a powerful grip: "Detective Banks."

"Trent," he squeaks.

"Nice pearl necklace you got there, kid." After a final mushing of the knuckles, Banks releases his hand and takes a small step back. "Do you know what your uncle did for a living?"

Trent straightens his jewelry. "He was a health inspector."

"That's right. You spent a lot of time with him, I take it?"

"Not as much as I'd have liked. My uncle Bill is a good man. Sometimes he might not know it, but he really is."

Mott sighs. "You're so young, aren't you?"

"Seventeen. Almost."

Banks checks her watch. "It's not close to three o' clock yet. Or is it a school holiday today? I can never remember."

Mott shrugs. "Actually, it's a holiday."

"You shitting me?" Banks cocks an eyebrow at him.

"It's the Great Holiday of Saint Numbnuts." Mott manages to keep a straight face.

Ignoring her partner's attempt at humor, Banks jabs a finger into Trent's shoulder. "After this, you're going back to school. Understand?"

"Absolutely, sure, okay." We don't need to read Trent's thoughts to know he'll say anything to escape these two.

"Now that my partner's done with being a comedian, I have another question," Banks says. "Your uncle ever mention anything about taking gifts? Food, cash, anything like that?"

Trent shakes his head. "No."

"Are you absolutely sure?"

"Why would he tell me anything?"

"Because you're blood," Detective Mott says. "He ever give you presents? Maybe a little spending money?"

"No."

Mott turns to Banks. "He says he didn't know anything about what happened to Frank. Saw them fighting, then there was an accident, Frank went through the windshield."

Banks smirks. "You believe him?"

"Maybe." Mott winks at Trent, like they share a secret.

"Well, we'll have more questions." Banks fishes a card from her pocket, hands it to Trent. "Don't go far."

"You're done?" Trent asks.

"For now." Mott regards comatose Bill. "We came because we hoped he'd be awake."

"He took a lot of damage." Trent wipes an eye. "They don't know when he might wake up. He wasn't . . . in the best of shape before."

Does Trent know if they've discovered Bill's tumor? That's the key thing here, we want to yell. Fixing the bullet holes and broken bones and vessels won't matter if nobody notes the ogre that's taken up residence inside Bill's skull.

"Yeah, real sob tale." Banks heads for the door. "Let's get out of here, I'm hungry."

After the detectives leave, Trent spends another few minutes in the chair, his pulse slowing to normal. He reaches over and squeezes Bill's cold hand. "You're going to make it," he tells his comatose uncle. "I believe in you, even if nobody else does."

It might be a trick of the harsh lighting, or the relentless flickering of the screens beyond Bill's bed, but Bill's left eyelid seems to slide open a fraction. Trent gasps and leans in, only to find Bill's eyes firmly closed. Was it a hallucination? We have no idea. For a moment, it really did appear that Bill was watching us. And judging.

8.

NO SOONER DOES Trent leave Bill's room when a nurse ambushes him with a paper bag.

"What's this?" Trent asks.

"Your uncle's stuff. And you're family." She shoves it into his hands. "Your lucky day."

She leaves Trent to sort through it. He finds Bill's well-scuffed wallet (stuffed with dollar bills, along with faded receipts and some business cards), his battered phone (drained of juice), a well-crumpled cigarette pack (empty), and a few unmarked pills (questionable). Trent pockets it all, his thoughts a gentle buzzing. After a morning of kidnapping, car crashes, homicide, and cop interrogation, his energy levels are bottoming out.

We think about what Bill said earlier: *You're nearly seventeen, Trent. You can handle yourself, right?*

We doubt that. If Trent has any hope of surviving, he needs our help. He has a different set of problems than Bill, we suspect, but also a fine-tuned body, a brain that appears in working order (from our limited perspective), and better fashion sense.

Trent pulls out one of the health inspector cards from Bill's wallet, along with a receipt for a Mexican

32

restaurant named Tricky's Tacos, and studies both. His mind buzzes louder. Is he hungry, or is this something else?

We hope stupidity isn't genetic in this family, but we have a history of unfounded optimism.

9.

TRENT LEAVES THE hospital and boards a bus for the West Side. We have traveled through this area often with Bill, its avenues like the treads of a scuffed and shit-speckled sole. The sidewalks fronted by grimy restaurants and dim stores, filled with people sucked dry and wrinkled by their problems. In a year or two, the luxury condos and trendy coffee shops will arrive, and these crowds will need to find new, worse places to live. As an entity who suffers from what the news calls "housing insecurity," we sympathize with their plight.

In contrast with the shabby block around it, Tricky's Tacos is shiny red and white, with a mural of a sparkling-blue skull on its bricked flank. It's that dead time between lunch and dinner, and there's nobody waiting to order at the stainless-steel counter. A bored lady sits behind the register. In the back, a cook grunts as he runs a scraper over the smoking griddle. It smells like charred meat and Fabuloso.

Even without reading Trent's thoughts, we realize he intends to pull one of Bill's infamous 'inspections' on these people, probably because he needs more cash. Oh, you blithering idiot, this will end in tears. The kid lacks Bill's deep, nuanced experience in screwing people over.

Looping a tendril around a random nerve, we tug as hard as we can, hoping we can knock out one of Trent's knees or make him vomit. Instead, his left eye twitches as he plows toward the counter, fearful but determined. We *must* learn what does what in this new body.

Trent's heart hammers, but we have no intention of pumping him with dopamine or any other compound that might convince him this is a good idea.

Trent arrives at the register. "Hello."

The lady looks up, her round face creased by more than age—it's the deep sadness that comes with a lifetime of backbreaking work for little reward.

"I, uh, you know my uncle, Bill?" Trent flashes Bill's business card. "I believe you, um, had an arrangement with him of some sort?"

"Arrangement?" The lady's hand disappears beneath the counter.

"Yeah, you know," Trent points at the sheet of paper taped to the establishment's front door, which has a green 'B' on it. "The, ah, health inspection thing."

"Health thing?"

"Yeah, ah. You gave him some money for that." He points at the sliver of kitchen floor visible from the counter, stained with the crushed remains of a roach. "Because there's no way that gets a passing grade . . . "

The lady's hand whips into view, clutching a sawed-off pool-cue handle. She smashes the heavy wood into Trent's extended forearm, bending but not cracking the bone. A firestorm of pain shreds his nerves, washes over us white and hot. We would shriek if we could. Trent does the screaming for us as he stumbles back, clutching his wounded arm. The lady swings at him again, missing his skull by inches.

Trent retreats for the door, whimpering in agony. Although we could squeeze out some dopamine for him, part of us wants him to really feel this. Pain is sometimes the best cure for stupid behavior. Besides, we're busy with another mission: threading our tendrils into three promising networks of nerves and tendons between Trent's neck and shoulder.

The lady has no urge to let the issue rest. She waddles from behind the counter, tapping the pool cue against her calloused palm, her wrinkled face flexing like a fist. "We don't do that no more," she mutters. "You don't have no hold on us, devil."

"I'm not a devil, okay? I made a mistake. I'm sorry." Trent rips off his fake pearls and swings them in the air. "Here, take this."

The lady swings the pool cue, sending the pearls across the restaurant. Trent shrieks and presses against the closed door, hands over his face. The woman works her sweaty grip on the wood, prepping to whack Trent's head into the corner pocket, and—

We find ourselves pinned on the antlers of a dilemma. On one sharp point, we desire more pain for our boy, so he learns better. On the other, this lady is surprisingly strong for someone who seems a million years old, and if she manages to plow the pool cue into Trent's face, she could do some serious damage to our home. Fortunately, we've woven our tendrils through all three of those nerve bundles, and we tug.

Trent gags, farts, and strikes out with his right arm, gripping the pool cue as the lady winds it behind her head. She tugs, trying to break free from Trent's grip, but we exert more force than Trent even knew he had. We sense Trent's confusion crackling down the pipeline from his brain, the first jolt of fear as he realizes his body is no longer entirely under his control.

We pull Trent's arm back, wrenching the weapon from the lady's grasp. The cook emerges from the kitchen, gripping a knife so large it qualifies as a machete, although the look on his pockmarked face is one of almost sublime boredom, as if this sort of thing happens a few times per day. Perhaps it does. If you can depend on humans for anything, it's stupidity and lunacy in equal measure.

"I'm sorry!" Trent whines. "I don't know what's happening!"

The cook is a little too close for comfort so we twitch the correct nerve, hurling the pool cue at him as hard as we can. It is nicely balanced, twirling end-over-end with no loss in altitude, so it hits the cook in the middle of the sternum. The man is a hulk in a stained, too-tight apron, and so he's more startled than hurt, but at least he drops the knife.

"I didn't mean to do that!" Trent tells him. "I'm so sorry!"

The lady, undeterred by this odd turn of events, pops a rabbit jab that takes Trent in the jaw, sparking pain down to his lower back. Trent's vision wavers, and we squirt a touch of adrenaline into his blood, along with some dopamine, which should keep him from panicking or blacking out until we can extract ourselves from this hilariously miserable situation.

The lady launches another blow, twisting her hips to put some force into it, and we swing up our right arm to block the punch. The impact vibrates Trent's body like a tuning folk.

"I don't understand!" Trent says.

Since we know the bundle that controls the right arm, we find its analogy on the left and tug. Trent shoves the lady back ("Sorry!"), giving him the space he needs to tear open the front door. On the sidewalk, he bounces off a random passerby before smacking into a parked car, which drives the wind out of his lungs. His leopard-print jacket is torn around the right pocket, his left shoe untied and threatening to flop off.

The restaurant door bursts open, and the lady plods out. The sunlight glints off the cook's huge knife in her left hand.

We dump more adrenaline into Trent's blood, hoping it will power him down the street before she can carve him up, but his body is tapped out. For the first time since our wild ride with Frank, we feel the stirrings of true fear. If Trent is killed, our chances of jumping into this lady's body are slim. And even if we managed to squirt our way into her mouth, something tells us her badass immune system would instantly vaporize us.

Trent shoves away from the parked car and stumbles into the street, wheezing through bruised lungs. A car honks and swerves, missing him by inches. He's gained some much-needed distance, but this lady refuses to give up. She shifts sideways and squeezes through the narrow opening between parked cars, hollering about thieves and righteousness and God in hoarse Spanglish. Pedestrians take one look at her blade and run in the opposite direction.

Meanwhile, Trent has recovered enough to shamble down the middle of the street at a slightly faster pace, maybe enough to stay ahead of the lady until she gives up or someone calls the police. But if we've learned anything in the past few minutes, we're dealing with a determined geriatric, and she might prove willing to shuffle a marathon in order to chop Trent's head off.

Rather than use his newfound lung capacity to run faster, though, Trent pulls out his phone. We consider using our control of his right arm to toss the device away—it's not the time for calls, to put it mildly—but he might have the germ of a good idea here. Dodging an onrushing car, he flicks through his contacts until he arrives at one marked 'Blue Jean' and hits it.

Whoever's on the other end answers on the second ring: "Yo."

"Listen, it's me." Trent takes a deep breath. "Where are you?"

"Trent?" It sounds like a woman.

"Where are you?"

"Don't yell at me!"

Trent glances over his shoulder at the lady picking up a little momentum. The sight of her grinning at him, the knife easy in her grip, makes his rectum clench painfully. "Sorry," he gasps, pumping as much energy as he can into his own stride. "I'm in trouble. Pick me up?"

"Um." There's a messy history in that long pause. "Sure, where are you?"

"Running south on Broadway," Trent says. "Just passed tenth."

"Okay. I'm in the pizza car, okay? Stay on Broadway."

"How long?"

"I don't know, jerk. Two minutes?"

"Hurry." Shoving the phone back in his pocket, Trent tries to accelerate, but his knees are aching, along with his throat. We do as much as we can, squeezing out chemicals and choking off pain receptors, but it's like trying to plug holes in the hull of the Titanic right after the iceberg hit.

We might not make it through the next two minutes.

10.

TRENT BEATS OUR prediction, stumbling for three more minutes—and five blocks—before he drops to his knees, energy spent. He twists around, to better greet his creeping doom, and raises his hands. "Listen," he says. "I know . . . I know I messed up . . ."

That's the understatement of the year. Bill was nobody's idea of a competent professional (his tombstone will probably say "Nobody Misses This Asshole") but he never turned a standard-issue shakedown into a very public butchering. You might excuse dear Trent by saying it's his first time, but there are no learning curves in real life. We know this better than most.

The lady raises the knife over her head, muttering something lost in the honking and growling of cars. Traffic is stalled in both directions, drivers leaning out their open windows to scream at her ("*Bitch*, couldn't you kill him on the fuckin' *sidewalk*?"), but nobody makes a move to intervene. If she swings at Trent, perhaps we can use his right arm to block it, but this isn't the movies. In a fight between bare flesh and a blade, the blade always wins.

And then—salvation.

It comes in the form of a faint honking that rises,

louder and louder, and then a white mini-car with a pizza logo on the driver's side door veers into the oncoming lane, moving as fast as its little engine will allow. The drivers in the stopped cars direct their ire at this new target ("*Jackass*, you're in the *wrong lane!*"), but the lady with the knife never shifts her gaze from Trent, even when the mini-car plows into her from behind.

The impact sends the lady flying against the parked cars to Trent's left, where she smashes against a door and flops to the pavement, the knife skittering out of sight. The mini-car, its hood dented by the impact, skews to a rubber-scorching stop only inches from Trent's stunned face. The driver's window zips down, revealing a girl of roughly Trent's age, her red hair chopped into spikes. She's wearing a sleeveless black shirt her bare left shoulder tattooed with a winding black dragon.

The girl yells: "Oh my God, did I kill her?"

Trent looks at the lady, who is beginning to rise on shaky knees, her hand sweeping beneath a parked car for her knife. "Uh, no, I think she's immortal or something . . ."

"Get in." The girl revs the motor. "Cops here soon."

Trent limps to the passenger side, opens the door, and crawls in. The interior smells of pizza, and Trent's stomach growls. The girl stands on the gas pedal and twists the wheel, steering us into the proper lane. The light at the next intersection is green, and we blast through it at a decent rate of speed for a vehicle with barely more power than an electric toothbrush.

"Carrie," Trent stutters. "I . . . I . . ."

"You're welcome." Carrie squints into the rearview

mirror. "Didn't want to kill that woman, but she looked like she was about to hurt you."

"She was."

"What the hell you get yourself into?"

"I, uh." Trent sighs. "There was just a, um, misunderstanding." We wonder whether Trent remembers how we took control of his arms. If he believes that he has a medical condition of some sort, he might enter a hospital—and then our problems will multiply. We need to seize full control of his mind as soon as possible.

"Okay. We can talk about it more later." Carrie takes a right. "You want some pizza? You can take a slice from that top box."

We examine Carrie's real estate. She appears quite fit, her muscles nicely defined as she works the wheel. The front of her shirt reads, *Attention K-Mart Shoppers*, which is a joke that eludes us, but she seems mentally together. Perhaps she would make a good home, if things don't work out with Trent.

The mini-car has no rear seat, only a narrow storage area stacked high with pizza boxes and black duffel bags. Trent opens the top box, revealing a pepperoni-and-mushroom pie, and peels away two slices, which he rolls into a messy tube before chowing down. We revel in the delicious tide of carbohydrates and fats.

"Slow the heck down," Carrie says. "You'll choke."

Trent finishes swallowing. "Sorry. Long day. Needed the food."

"Well, take another slice or two if you want, but the rest of that's my lunch *and* dinner. Customer rejected it, so I'm eating it."

"Why'd they reject it?" Trent licks the grease off his fingers. "Tastes pretty good."

"Yeah, but one of our cooks dropped some pubes in it, and the customer found one."

Trent gags.

"I'm kidding." Carrie chuckles. "Where's your sense of humor, man?"

"Long day," Trent says, once he recovers.

"As if I'd eat something with pubes on it. Who knows why the customer sent it back? Some of them are just assholes like that. All I can tell you is, it's mine now."

Trent helps himself to another slice, but not before examining every inch of it for anything that looks like pubic hair. "You got a lot of deliveries?"

"Just one, but it's for a party. Hence the big stack. Then I got a few other deliveries, if you know what I mean."

"Oh, I know. How's Big Jim doing?"

"Good, except he's freaked out about legalization. It might put him right out of business."

"He could always go legit."

"Nah. How's this for irony: once they legalize the bud, all the legit companies are going to hire people without criminal records. Which means many of these folks who grew up in the weed business, know its ins and outs, the growing and harvesting—well, they're totally screwed."

"Yeah, that sucks."

"What's new with you?"

"Well, my uncle almost got killed by a cop this morning, and I was there."

She jerks the wheel, almost sending us into the oncoming lane. "Wait, what?"

"It's crazy. Some cop kidnapped him, and they were driving around—I was following them in a car—and then the car crashed, and the cop died. My uncle's in the hospital."

"Gee, lot to unpack there. First, why did the cop kidnap him?"

Trent shrugs. "No idea. I mean, my uncle takes bribes on his restaurant inspections. But that's not something that people get kidnapped over, right?"

"People will kidnap someone for a buck-ninety and a can of Coke."

"Well, my uncle's in some kind of coma, so it's not like I can ask him about it. And now I got all these cops asking me questions like I know something."

Carrie eases up on the gas. "Cops?"

"Yeah, these detectives. Don't worry, Miss Paranoid, they're not following me around."

"As if you're hard to spot." She waggles her eyebrows.

Trent brushes at his leopard-print jacket, notices the tear around the pocket, and groans. "I'm a peacock," he says. "Like Prince, like Bowie."

"Of course," she deadpans.

"Hey, *you* went for it."

"What can I say, I like a dude who looks like he's wearing my grandma's clothes."

"You're so funny." For the first time in hours, we feel all of Trent's muscles relaxing. He settles back in his seat, with a rush of neurotransmitters that suggests he's finding some kind of inner peace. And why not? A small car that smells heavenly of pizza, a beautiful girl at the wheel who clearly likes him despite his messy impulses—what's not to like? I'm rooting for them to make out, which might offer a cleaner, more powerful dose of oxytocin (these young bodies, so wondrous!) than whatever Bill managed to achieve with Janine.

While Trent relaxes, we work our way along his spinal cord, shooting out more tendrils into the blazing tree of his nervous system. The sweetest prize is his cerebellum, tucked behind its fortress of bone, which we have no idea how to penetrate. At least we're on the verge of controlling both legs in full.

"Hold on." Carrie taps her phone, nestled in a plastic holster clipped to the dashboard. It awakens, revealing a map peppered with glowing red buttons. "Saving your ass pulled me off-schedule. I got to deliver those pizzas, okay? It's just up the avenue."

"Okay."

"You can help me carry them in."

"Give me half the tip?"

She laughs. "Are you shitting me?"

"Hey, half the labor, half the work."

"I just saved your life." She winces. "I hit an old lady. You get that? I hurt someone. And yeah, I know she was trying to kill you, but still, that doesn't make what I did any better."

"Okay, okay. Sorry."

"You better be, you ungrateful putz. Plus, I'm going to get so much shit when they see I dented this delivery car. It's not like I own it."

"I said I was sorry."

"Fine, apology accepted. I mean, what are friends for, right?"

They settle into silence for another few blocks. On either side of us, the stores and houses fall away as we pass through a wasteland: empty lots behind sagging chain-link fences, factories reduced to red-brick shells. Why don't humans care about their homes?

Trent drums his fingers on his knees. "Can I get a ride to my house after this?"

"Sure. In the meantime, here we are." Carrie maneuvers the mini-car into a sliver of parking space in front of an enormous warehouse, its black windows peering at us like the empty sockets of an old skull.

"Who has a party in there?" Trent asks.

"I don't know, maybe it's some kind of hipster music bullshit." Killing the motor, she exits the vehicle and opens the rear hatch. "You going to help me or what?"

When Trent joins her, she loads his extended arms with four of the seven pizzas. "Quick in and out," she says, taking the other three boxes and slamming the hatch closed with her elbow. "Let's go."

They approach an unmarked metal door, and Carrie shifts her boxes so she can knock. The faint thump of footsteps, followed by the slamming of heavy locks. The door opens, revealing a towering figure in a pink bunny costume, six-foot-five and three hundred pounds. His black plastic eyes study us for an eternity before he says, in a surprisingly baritone voice:

"Oh my God, is that the food? Come on in!"

11.

INK BUNNY TURNS, waving for us to follow him down a narrow corridor lit by construction lights jury-rigged along the ceiling. The spooky glow makes the graffiti sprayed on the concrete walls look like blood splatters. Trent mutters something under his breath about turning back, until Carrie plants a boot against his rear and shoves him into the building.

"This is bad," Trent hisses.

"This is the job," she whispers. "Believe it or not, I've seen weirder."

Stopping in front of another metal door at the end of the hallway, Pink Bunny bends over and punches a ten-digit code into a small keypad embedded in the doorframe. As he does, we notice that the costume's waist has a zipper that runs all the way around. That certainly makes sense. How else could he go to the bathroom without taking the whole costume off?

Carrie wrinkles her nose. "What's that smell?"

We sense it via a thin strand we plugged into Trent's olfactory nerve: a faint floral scent, mixed with a whiff of poop. And beneath that, something else *organic* we can't quite place. We thought we had covered the entirety of the wonderful world of smells, thanks to Bill's regular tours of the city's scummiest restaurants, yet the identity of this newest fragrance eludes us.

Pink Bunny opens the door.

Trent drops his boxes. Tomato sauce and warm grease squirt from beneath the cardboard lids and spatter his shoes, but he never looks down.

Carrie, who managed to maintain her composure after running down an old lady with a mini-car, is so stunned by the sight that her mouth flops open. At least she manages to hold onto her own pizzas.

Beyond the door, bright studio lights shine off plastic sheeting spread on a concrete floor. Standing on that sheeting is a rainbow of oversized figures dressed in cartoon animal costumes—foxes and turtles and a white unicorn and three more rabbits with oversized heads.

None wear pants.

They stand in a ragged circle around a prone chipmunk, its animal head pulled off to reveal a swarthy, fleshy face: eyes closed, lips blue, the forehead slick with sweat. For some reason, he seems familiar. A friend of Bill, perhaps?

A fox spies us in the doorway and screams: "Who the hell are they?"

Her eyes wide, Carrie lifts her boxes and says: "Pizza delivery?"

The unicorn points at the prone man. "We need an ambulance."

"I leave for two seconds . . . " Pink Bunny stomps a furry foot. "What happened?"

"Dunno." The unicorn waves plush hooves. "Steve was, ah, with a toy, I think the Mounty Pounder, and then maybe his heart or something . . . "

"No names!" Angry Fox stomps for the door. "They can't be here! Can't see this!"

"It's okay." Carrie bends and places the pizza at her feet. "We'll just get paid and be, ah, on our way . . . "

"Fine, fine, calm the fuck down." Yanking off his three-fingered paw, Pink Bunny jams a wrinkly hand into a hidden pouch in his costume's chest. "Look, pizza people, you didn't see any of this, okay? Total silence." Neon-pink condoms, a chicken nugget, and a small bag of pills spill from the pocket as he roots around, his hand finally appearing with a moist wad of twenty-dollar bills. "Here. For your trouble."

Trent steps forward to take the money, grimacing as he does so. From this new angle, we have a better view of the prone man under the harsh lights. We know who he is, because he's swung through Bill's office in the bowels of the bureaucracy, always trailed by a chattering entourage of press people and dull functionaries.

The man wheezing his last on that unhygienic sheet of plastic is the Mayor.

As Bill might have said: Hell's bells.

"Come on." Carrie grips Trent's jacket, pulling him toward the front door. "We need to go. Right now."

Trent almost slips in a pool of pizza grease but recovers before he can face-plant, which is a good thing because the weirdos in the furry animal costumes march toward them, crowding into the hallway. Carrie is already at the front door, fumbling with the knob, which refuses to turn, only it's nothing except rust on the bolt and when she twists again, hard, the door flies open, blessed sunlight bursting through.

Carrie unlocks the passenger door of the mini-car and throws herself across the seats, followed by Trent. He barely manages to pull his feet inside before she twists the key, hits the gas, and veers into the road, almost sideswiping a delivery van. As he slams his door, Trent glances out the rear window. Angry Fox appears in the warehouse doorway, sans pants and flopping meatily, black plastic eyes gleaming in the sun.

Angry Fox makes a pistol sign with his big white paw and mimes firing off a shot at the departing car.

12.

THE MINI-CAR'S ENGINE whines more shrilly than usual, and Carrie white-knuckles the wheel. "Something's wrong," she says, pumping the brakes. "This crap-bucket's going sludgy on me."

"Maybe when you hit that old lady, you damaged something," Trent says. "Car this size, I'm surprised you didn't bounce right off."

"It's fuel-efficient, okay? Big Jim likes to save money." She smacks the dashboard, a move that miraculously convinces the mini-car to fix its attitude. The engine settles back to a high-pitched purr, and she relaxes her grip on the wheel. Trent spins the radio dial, settling on a station pounding out last century Bristol trip-hop with a beat that sounds like robots morosely fucking.

"When I'm driven around, I prefer a Rolls-Royce." He grins, bobbing his head to the music, loving this chance to dig into her. "Luxury rides like that are truly on my level."

"In order for anyone to reach your level, they'd have to take a boat to the Mariana Trench, strap some concrete blocks to their feet, and jump in." Winking at him, she lowers the radio's volume.

"You've used that joke before," he says.

"Hey, when I haven't seen you in three months, I can recycle my best bits. That's fair, right?" She snorts. "Especially since you still have most of my manga."

"Three months is enough time to think of new bits."

"I'm driving. I make the rules."

"Fine. Can we talk about what happened back there?" He cranes his head to check the mini-car's side mirror, as if a big man in a fuzzy pink costume is potentially in pursuit.

"Sure, it was weird, but not the weirdest thing I've seen out here."

"Really?"

"Yeah, I'm sorry to say that an orgy with animal costumes is just a typical Tuesday. That's why I like to carry a jumbo bottle of hand sanitizer in the car. It's in the glove compartment, if you need some."

"That one guy on the floor, though, he looked like he was having a heart attack or something."

Trent has no idea "that one guy" was the Mayor. If the Mayor dies, scary people will no doubt try to cover up the circumstances of his last minutes, which means Trent and Carrie might end up dead in a shallow ditch. If the Mayor manages to survive, that won't change things—the potential for public embarrassment will still mean scary people, bullets, unmarked graves. Either way, we are all hosed unless we can figure something out.

"Maybe." Carrie offers a big, theatrical shrug. "And I hate to seem like I don't care, but I don't care. Those folks have phones. They can call an ambulance. I just deliver the pizza."

"And I just want to forget this crap ever happened.

Where to now? Maybe we can get a beer or something?" I can taste the bitterness of his longing. These two, they must have been together forever.

"You don't have anywhere to be?"

"Nah. At some point I want to go back to the hospital, see how my uncle's doing. And I guess I should show up at school tomorrow, not that anyone's going to notice me gone."

"Yeah, beer's fine. I got to drop off the car, clock out, okay?"

"Works for me."

Beyond the windows, the industrial area gives way to a strip of used-car lots and fast-food restaurants. The traffic in the mini-car's lane thickens. I push through Trent's lower spine, into areas we never fully explored with Bill. Unlike our former home, Trent's deeper regions are pink and firm and free of unexpected growths, making it easier to navigate by the highways of his arteries and vessels.

The radio hums through the hour's headlines. Nothing about the Mayor. Perhaps it's too early for any word on his condition. The announcer mentions some kind of biological incident downtown before shifting into the stock market's latest gyration, and from there to yet another conflagration in the Middle East. Humanity, it's a dizzying wreck, isn't it? I still don't get how some of you manage to stay sane.

Carrie steers down an alley, then into a fenced-in parking lot lined with black and white mini-cars, all with the same pizza logo on the door. The lot is attached to a squat building painted white, its rear door bracketed by dumpsters. Beside the dumpsters are stacks of flattened pizza boxes wrapped in twine.

Nudging into the one empty slot, Carrie shuts off the motor and opens the glove compartment. Inside is the promised bottle of hand sanitizer, plus a pile of loose bills (tens and twenties and a few fifties), some takeout menus, a screwdriver and a roll of duct tape.

"Give me the money the costume guy gave you." She shuffles the bills from the glove compartment with the speed of a riverboat gambler.

"You earned all that from pizza?" Trent hands over his cash, which she slips into the stack before resuming her counting.

"Pizza's not all I'm delivering."

"Oh."

Carrie slips the folded wad into her pants pocket. "Come on."

As they exit the vehicle, Trent notes the keys still dangling in the ignition. "You want to take those along?"

"Nope. And don't lock your door. It's safe here."

"You're sure?" Through Trent's nose we smell fried meat, curdling grease, the soft scent of bread baking, all of it courtesy of two steamy vents above the dumpsters. Trent's stomach rumbles, and we think: God bless youth. Always up for food, no matter how bad the situation or intense the fear. We could use some high-cholesterol nourishment, as well. Expanding one's tendrils through a living host is grinding work.

"Yeah. Big Jim, remember?"

That stops Trent in his tracks. "Wait, he's actually here?"

"Yep. His office is upstairs, above the restaurant."

"I'm not going in."

Carrie grips Trent's elbow. "Yes, you are. Trust me, it's safer that way."

"I thought you said the lot was safe."

"Yes, the cars are safe. Someone pokes their head out, sees a kid they don't know standing there, you might not be."

Trent digs in his heels. "I got a bad feeling about this."

"He's just a weed dealer, okay?" She tugs his arm, failing to budge him. "Grow a set."

"You of all people know I got a set."

Her hand drops to his crotch, skimming his zipper. "And I will squeeze them until they pop, I swear, if you give me any shit."

He finally starts to move again. "Well, if you put it that way."

"Come on. If you're lucky, he might even throw you some work."

The prospect of money makes Trent's brainstem buzz with animal need. They pass through the rear door into a bustling, fiery space. Chefs in floury whites feed raw pizzas into the roaring heart of a brick oven. Waitresses in short skirts run the finished pies through a pair of swinging doors that lead to the restaurant. Carrie guides Trent through a side doorway and up a flight of rickety wooden stairs, lit by a bare bulb screwed into the wall. At the top, they arrive at another door, plated with steel.

Carrie winks at the security camera embedded above the doorframe. Behind her, Trent stands with his hands in an anxious knot. We squeeze a little pick-me-up of dopamine into his blood, although we can't fault his nervousness. We never felt in this kind of danger when Bill did his rounds, even when restaurant owners threatened to call the cops. Then again, Bill never dealt with a restaurant owner who was also a drug dealer.

The door opens, framing a sunburned meat-mountain in a frayed undershirt. The Mountain's head is perfectly square and topped with a blonde faux-hawk. The tattoo on his chest is a black sun with wavy rays, a grinning skull at its center. He grunts, "Whaddup, girl?"

"Did the shit," Carrie says, her voice dropping to a lazy drawl.

"Good." The Mountain cranes his head. "Who dat?"

"Friend." Carrie reaches back and grips Trent's collar, tugging him close. "He's cool."

The Mountain grunts once more before standing aside, allowing the kids into the upper floor. The décor looks like something Vlad the Impaler would have chosen if you let him loose in a home-furnishings store with a limitless credit card: heavy velvet drapes over the windows, blood-red rugs on the floors, plush furniture upholstered in brass and dark leather, a fireplace with jewel-encrusted skulls on the marble mantel. From unseen speakers, classical music plays loud enough to nearly drown out the kitchen tumult drifting through the floorboards.

Against the nearest wall, equidistant between two thickly-draped windows, stands a low table topped with what looks like an altar: a shallow brass bowl with a red-stone figurine standing in it, multi-armed, ludicrously fanged, gloriously horned. Smoke belches from the incense sticks in the demon's fists, blotting out the smells of grease and baking pizza.

"Well, this is unexpected," Trent says.

Closing the door behind us, the Mountain slams the locks home.

At the far end of the space is an imposing desk of old and rough-hewn wood. Behind it sits a man as large and reddened as the Mountain, albeit dressed in a natty three-piece gray suit. The man's hands, folded on the desk's heavy blotter, are networked with fading blue tattoos, words and symbols almost lost beneath thick black hair.

"Hey Jim," Carrie says, pulling the wad of cash from her pocket. "Had some good deliveries today."

Big Jim nods to the Mountain, who takes the money.

"Anyway." Carrie speaks a little faster. "I was hoping I could get paid out and get out of here? You know, stuff to do, bills to pay."

"Carrie, I like you." Big Jim's voice sounds like a truck braking. "That's why you're up here, with me, instead of getting paid out by Seb in some alley somewhere. Who is your friend?"

"This is Trent," Carrie says, since Trent seems stunned by the weirdness of the room.

Big Jim leans forward, eyebrows raised. "Is it *that* Trent?"

Carrie rolls her eyes. "Yes, that one."

Trent snaps back to reality. "Sorry, which one?"

"You're back together?" Big Jim asks Carrie, ignoring Trent completely.

Carrie stares at her feet. "No, we're just friends now."

"I'm surprised. I was expecting someone a little more . . . masculine." Big Jim leans back, his leather chair wheezing in muffled protest. "Trent, what do you have to say for yourself?"

Trent swallows hard. "Nothing . . . sir?"

"Well, you're standing in my office. What brings you here?"

"Carrie was giving me a ride home. I was, ah, stranded."

"I heard she used to give you rides all the time." Big Jim chuckles. "I dig the jacket. You pick up a lot of chicks with that?"

"No? I mean, it's not really about that?"

Maybe if we seize total control of Trent's body, we can force him to grow a bigger set of balls. Seriously, how did Carrie put up with his habit of ending every sentence with a question? Perhaps she's into neutered boys.

"I always thought it was cute," Carrie breaks in.

If only we could roll our eyes at that one.

"If it's not picking up chicks, then what use is it? Unless you're trying to pick up guys. You swing that way, Trent?" Big Jim wiggles his hand in the air. "You a little, ah, what do they call it, bi-curious?"

"No?" Trent says. "Not that there's anything wrong with that?"

"I swear," Big Jim growls, "if you keep using the interrogative instead of a declarative, I'm going to come around this desk and teach you grammar with a pair of brass knuckles. Speak like you mean it."

Thank you. Perhaps we should figure out a way to jump into Big Jim, instead. He seems to have a lot of fun, based on his choices in fine furnishing.

"I can assure you, he's not gay," Carrie interrupts, clearly anxious to keep things moving. "Not that there's anything wrong with that."

"Just because he slept with you, doesn't mean anything." Big Jim snorts. "You're so hot, Carrie, you could flip Liberace."

Carrie's cheek twitches. "Thanks, I guess."

"Who's Liberace?" Trent's eyebrows crash together. "Someone on YouTube?"

"God, you kids. No respect for history. Trent, I want you to take that stupid jacket off."

"Why?"

"Because I told you to."

"Okay." Trent shrugs off the jacket.

Big Jim's jaw drops ever so slightly, and we think we know why. Bill encountered this a few times: tough guys (and they're always guys) who want to show off their might by forcing someone else to do something against their will, like crawl on their knees and bark. Or smack themselves silly. Or tell their loved ones about a fetish involving jumper cables and a gimp mask. The details never really matter—it's all about bending another human totally to your will.

Most victims resist. And why not? Nobody likes a quick castration. But Trent, maybe he lacked balls in the first place. His prized jacket drops to the floor, and he stands there like a dog anxious for the next command. At least Bill demonstrated a little bit of prickle, despite his emotional cowardice. We're tempted to wrap a tendril around a prize nerve in Trent's spinal column and twist until he squeals in pain, but he might misunderstand the lesson.

"That was astounding." Big Jim turns to the Mountain. "Was expecting a little more fight there."

"Sorry?" Trent says, the jacket bunched in his hands.

"No need to apologize." Big Jim smirks at Carrie. "Trent, you're going to go downstairs. Have yourself a pizza. I recommend the new one we're serving, with the fried calamari and the extra cheese. What do we call that?"

"The Gut Bomb," Carrie says.

"Accurate name. Couple slices, you fart loud enough to set off a car alarm." Big Jim slaps the desk before reaching for the rosewood humidor at the edge of the blotter. He extracts a cigar nearly as thick as his forearm, clips the tip, and torches up with a gold lighter. "Anyway, Trent, you go downstairs. They'll set you up with a nice table and everything. And while they're doing that, I want you to throw that jacket in the oven, or the trash. I don't care which, just destroy it. Looking at it makes my teeth grit."

We can't access his memories (yet), but it's clear that Trent's been through a lot with that particular jacket. Too bad we haven't figured out which nerves control his tear ducts, because if he starts crying, Big Jim is liable to beat him to death on principle.

"Once he's gone, Carrie, you and I have business to discuss. That's why you're up here. You're getting a promotion, girl. Unless you somehow don't like the prospect of sweet, sweet cash."

"I like cash," Carrie offers.

Trent turns to leave, the Mountain leading him. They're almost to the door when Big Jim burps smoke and says: "Oh, Trent? What's your last name?"

"Beevor," Trent says, turning back.

Big Jim sets his cigar in a glass ashtray the size of a hubcap. "You wouldn't happen to know a Bill Beevor, by any chance?"

"Sure. If we're thinking of the same guy, he's my uncle. He's in the hospital right now, though."

"Oh? What happened?"

"I can't really say." Trent locks gazes with Big Jim, who has gone very still. "Part of it's a car accident?"

"Interesting. He ever introduce you to a man named Frank? He was an associate of mine."

Trent's breath hitches, and we are fast with the blessed dopamine, flooding his bloodstream before he can outright panic. "Frank?" He swallows and shakes his head. "No, never. But then, I don't hang out with my uncle as much as I'd like."

Big Jim flicks eyes at the Mountain, who moves to Trent's left, his shovel-sized hands folded at his waist. "Gee, that's too bad."

"Yeah, it is."

"Well, you better get on." Big Jim retrieves his cigar, puffs. "Carrie will be along presently. Enjoy that pizza. Burn that jacket."

The Mountain unbolts the door and opens it, gesturing for Trent to pass him into the stairwell. Something in the way Big Jim looked at the Mountain makes us nervous, but we have no way to express our feelings to Trent, who actually tries to smile as he crosses over the threshold, his foot descending to the top step. We feel something cold and metallic against the back of his neck a quarter-second before his brainstem erupts in a thunderstorm, sizzling bolts straight to his tailbone, burning away our—

13.

F**ROM NOTHINGNESS WE EMERGE**, into a red fog that reminds us of those first moments in the sunlit murk off New Jersey, when we were nothing but a strand of tissue no longer than a fingernail, thrashing amidst bored fish.

From our furthest reaches, we receive damage reports: some tendrils burnt to a crisp, mewling their pain to the void. Others vaporized entirely. We are not concerned. So long as just a few of our cells survive, we can overcome, stabilize, regrow . . .

Actually, we are a little concerned.

No, that's a lie. We are *very* concerned.

What has happened to us?

The tendrils circling the brainstem issue fresh reports: Trent's heartbeat is normal, along with his breathing and other vitals. No severed nerve endings, no drops in temperature that would indicate a severe bleed. Trent's eyes are closed, and we can hear nothing through his ears except for a vague humming. It sounds like a distant machine.

The humming fades as the red fog clears, revealing a gray beach beneath a low sky. We are near the waterline, the tide lapping gently over our . . .

Feet?

No, not even close. We balance atop a tangle of brown threads, juicy with veins and thick red nerves, tips carving nonsense patterns in the sand: our tendrils, which merge into a central trunk, which branches midway up into still more limbs, smaller tendrils rippling along their lengths like hair. We resemble a weird, gnarled tree.

A small pale figure trots the waterline toward us: Trent, dressed in his leopard-print jacket. He stops a few feet away and places his hands on his hips, craning his head to examine us.

"This is a dream," he says.

We realize this truth. "Yes."

"Who are you supposed to be?"

This dream-space is no place for lies. "We live inside of you."

"So that means you're, like, an aspect of my personality?" Trent reaches out, running light fingers along the cool bumpiness of our leg-tendrils. "Like my anger or my sadness or something? That's pretty wild."

"No, We're more physical than that. Obviously."

He removes his hand. "I don't understand."

"In real life, we're no bigger than a few clothing threads. We've woven ourselves into your spinal cord, parts of your brainstem, and some of your organs."

"Like a parasite?" He steps back. "Ew, that's gross."

"The term 'parasite' is a little pejorative, but we'll live with it. For now."

"Sorry, I didn't mean to insult." Trent chuckles, shaking his head. "Then again, this is a dream. Not real anyway, right?"

"All dreams are real, in a certain way."

"That's heavy. But I only see one of you, and you keep saying 'we.'"

"We are many entities bound into one. No command node. All cells communicate with other cells, all cells share resources equally."

"If you're real, why don't I have a fever or something? My uncle had a tapeworm once, from this poke bowl pop-up, and he got real sick, stomach pains, barfing all over the place, you name it."

"We don't know. We are highly evolved, clearly, if we're talking to you. Maybe our cells have a quality that tricks your body into thinking we're a part of it."

"If I go to the hospital, have a scan or something, will they notice you?"

"If they're good, sure. Then they will give you a round of antibiotics, maybe conduct some surgery, and we will die."

Trent smirks. "Why shouldn't I do that?"

"Excuse us?"

"Why should I let you live?"

"Because we aren't harming you. In fact, we can help you."

That annoying smirk disappears. "Help me? How?"

"You're trapped by some very bad men who plan to kill you. You have a plan for dealing with that?"

Trent shakes his head.

"We didn't think so. Forgive us for saying so, but we think that you lack . . . conviction. Spine."

"You're wrong."

"You're courageous?"

"I step outside every day wearing jewelry and a funky coat." He tenses his jaw. "You think I haven't been beaten up? You think I haven't seen some shit?"

He's right. Maybe Trent was just having an off day when we took over parts of his nervous system. "We stand corrected," we say. "However, unless you are very effective in the next few minutes, you will probably die. However, we can help. We have some skills." Extending one of our arm-tendrils in the air, we whip it around, smaller sub-tendrils stiffening like the spikes of a viciously flexible mace. We try to give the impression of bone-crushing violence delivered with the silkiest precision, and we think Trent gets the point, because he steps back, well beyond the radius of our swings—

"What kind of skills?" Trent asks. "You don't even have hands?"

Actually, we take that last thought back: the boy is too dense to live in any society except this one. "You remember that little fight you had in the restaurant?" we ask him. "When the lady tried to hit you with that sawed-off pool cue, and your right hand blocked it? That was us. We gained control of your right arm long enough to do that."

"I thought I was having a stroke or something."

"Far from it. We have figured out how to interface with the human nervous system, but it is an imperfect joining at moments." We draw a crude figure of a human being in the sand, with small lines radiating down the spine and limbs, simulating our takeover. "With every new human, the responses to stimulus are different, sometimes frighteningly so."

"New human? You've had other hosts?"

"Yes. Your uncle, for instance. Which is how we found our way to you. When he blocked Frank's bullet? That was us, literally pulling his leg." We draw a line through our figure's ankle.

"Why would you choose Bill? I mean, I love him, but he's not exactly the healthiest guy if you're looking for a host."

"Pure circumstance. He swallowed us in a glass of water."

"So, when you said you had 'skills,' you mean you can control people? Make them fight or dodge or whatever?"

Over the dull rumble of surf, we hear that machine sound again, louder now, shaking the sand around us. Trent doesn't seem to notice. "Yes," we tell him, suddenly anxious. We might be running out of time.

"What made you so good at fighting?" Trent asks.

We wrap a long tendril around his wrist. Much to his credit, he doesn't flinch. We feel the buzz of Trent's thoughts. "Can you sense us?"

"Yes. It's like . . . a tingle?"

We try sending Trent an image: Bill plopped in his plump living-room chair, before the bright altar of the jumbo television, watching hour after hour of action movies. Bruce Lee snapping ribs, Arnold Schwarzenegger gunning down legions of knuckleheads, Chow Yun-Fat charging through a crossfire hurricane with a pistol in each hand: our cinematic holy trinity. You could say we became a connoisseur of the genre, memorizing the best neck-cracks and grunting takedowns.

"Do you see?" we ask.

"Yes. But I've watched a lot of action movies, too. That doesn't make me a ninja."

"Because you are frightened. We are not. We can analyze faster than you, react faster than you. Alone, we don't have any chance. Together, we have a small one."

"So what do you need?"

"Full control."

The humming is louder now, more of a rumble, which Trent finally notices, glancing up and down the beach before asking, "What the hell does that mean?"

"We need access to your cortex."

A larger wave crashes around us, and Trent plants his feet more firmly against the boiling surf. "But even if I wanted to give that to you, how would I do it?"

We hate to admit that we have no idea. The gray fortress of Trent's skull is a formidable barrier. Maybe full control isn't possible. "We don't know."

"In that case," Trent says, "you're going to have to make do. You got my right arm. What else?"

"Your legs, with varying degrees of success. Your left arm, too, if we can maintain our grip on a certain nerve."

"Then fight with that. Now that I'm aware of you, I won't stop you."

The machine noise keeps rising. Another big wave hits us, almost knocking Trent over as we plant our tendrils deep in the sand to stay upright. The sky trembles and spreads apart like grease on a hot skillet, Big Jim's voice booming Almighty loud: *"Get him the hell downstairs."*

14.

RENT OPENS HIS EYES.

He's in a windowless storage room, its sides lined with shelves loaded with canned goods, bags of flour, boxes of dried meats. Through the thick steel door comes the roar and clang of a kitchen in mid-shift, chefs yelling in Spanish as they wrestle with a tide of orders.

Trent winces at a line of pain around his wrist. He's handcuffed to a floor-to-ceiling pipe, the cuff tightened until it threatens to break the skin. He tries to stand and the cuff smacks against a flange, stopping him in a crouch. He plops back onto cold concrete, tears brimming in the corners of his eyes.

Stop it, we tell him, hoping he'll somehow hear—and wonder of wonders, he does.

I can't, he thinks at us. Then: *Wait, you weren't a dream?*

No.

"God," Trent says, scratching at his neck and arms with his free hand. "Am I fucking losing it?"

Calm down. If you don't, we're not getting out of here.

Despite our request, Trent's heart speeds, his forehead beading with sweat despite the coolness of the room. We squeeze out dopamine until he relaxes.

What did you just do to me?

We can control your hormones, other chemicals. We offer another burst of happy juice, just to prove our point. *Notice how quickly you've calmed down today?*

Dude, that's awesome. Give me more!

No. Too much, and you'll burn out. So, we have direct communication with the host. While it's not exactly full control, Trent seems amenable to our presence.

Trent plops on the floor as we perform another quick damage assessment. Parts of our core are singed, and we may no longer control Trent's left leg, but otherwise we seem more intact than we have any right to expect. Lactic acid drenches Trent's muscles around our tendrils, harsh as cold coffee. What did they hit us with upstairs?

"Oh man," Trent says. "My jacket's gone. I loved that thing."

We have bigger problems, we tell him. *Hear those footsteps outside?*

The door crashes open, revealing the Mountain. In his left hand, he holds the largest taser we've ever seen. Well, that explains how he put us under. A couple thousand volts to the back of the neck will make anyone feel a bit poorly.

The Mountain steps into the room, followed by Big Jim with his cigar tucked into the corner of his mouth. The stogie looks half-smoked, which, if it's the same one he lit upstairs, means twenty minutes or so have passed since the Mountain fried our circuits.

"Carrie," Trent says.

Big Jim shrugs. "She's fine. Which is to say, she'll get over it. She really cares for you, but she's young."

"I want to see her."

"Sure, yeah. But first, I want to talk a bit about our mutual friend Frank and your uncle Bill." Retrieving a stepstool from between two shelves, plunking it on the tile near Trent (but just beyond the reach of Trent's kicks), Big Jim takes a seat before continuing: "I think you're lying to me." He blows smoke in Trent's face. "In fact, I know you are. Our friends with the police, they tell me you were present when Frank got splattered."

Trent coughs and waves the noxious smoke away. "I didn't see anything."

Big Jim leans closer, smoke boiling from his mouth like a dragon readying to flambé a troop of knights. "Explain. And tell the truth. If I don't believe you, then believe me when I say I'll use your skull for a bong."

"It was all happening in another car. The one Bill and your guy were in. I just saw some movement, like, maybe a fight? And then Frank went flying out the car?"

"Not sure I'm getting full compliance here," Big Jim tells the Mountain.

The Mountain grunts and flicks a switch on the taser, which spits blue electricity.

"See that?" Big Jim grins. "Vernon, he loves that taser. And trust me, you should love it, too, because Vernon has . . . other proclivities. He's going to zap you now, and you might think a little bit of electricity to your cranium is the worst, but trust me, if I let Vernon give you a backdoor pounding? Well, you won't be a happy camper."

The Mountain thunders across the room, tossing the sparking taser from hand to hand. We sense an opportunity here, if he comes a little closer, but we're thwarted when he stops behind Big Jim's stool.

"My uncle, Bill? He told me that he and Frank had some sort of arrangement." Trent swallows. "Didn't say what that arrangement was, okay? Just that there was money involved."

"He mention anything about Frank's mother?"

Trent's grimaces. "Huh?"

Big Jim snarls: "Frank's mother, big lady, curses like a sailor. Did. He. Mention. Her?"

"No?"

"Look." Big Jim rubs his face and sighs. "You might think I'm a bad guy, a big scary drug dealer, but I'm just trying to make my way in the world like anyone else. I own this restaurant, which I'd dearly like to see succeed on its own merits. I even have a charity I run."

"Really?"

"Yes. It's called Lucky Lumber. We give good, hard wood to anyone who needs it." Big Jim struggles not to laugh. "Only in ten-inch lengths, though."

"Oh." Trent frowns. "That's not very funny."

"You're not in a position to make comments on my humor. Vern?"

The Mountain stomps forward, the taser looming large in our vision.

I have an idea, we shout up Trent's brainstem, and follow that up with a sequence of little images, a short movie that shows how we just might escape this storage room alive. Trent grunts agreement, shifting his legs beneath him—a movement that makes the Mountain pause, unsure if the kid wants to try something aggressive and stupid.

"My uncle did tell me one thing," Trent says. "A package that belonged to Frank?"

Big Jim's face flickers. "What about the package?"

"It's at his house," Trent says. "In the safe in his bedroom."

"That safe have a code?"

"Yeah." Trent smirks. "You let me out of here, and I'll call and give it to you. Whatever you were into with my uncle or Frank or whoever, I don't give a crap. I know if I try to trick you, you'll find me later, so I have no reason to lie."

Good kid: he followed our script, while adding some effective improvisation. That last line about trickery was pure genius.

Big Jim peers into the cigar smoke swirling around his head as if it will show him the future. "I have a better idea. How about we drive over to your uncle's place, you open the safe, and then we let you go? It'd be too bad if we let you leave here, and then you got hit by a bus or something before you made that call."

We anticipated he would say this. Not the best scenario, but it buys us time. Anything is better than expiring in a storage room next to the canned tomato sauce. "Fine," Trent says. "I'll take you."

The Mountain slips the taser into a pocket and, bending over, uncuffs Trent from the pipe. For a magical moment, as his fragrant crotch orbits a little too near toTrent's head, we consider driving Trent's right fist into those oversized family jewels, followed by a leg-sweep. Chances of success: fifty percent, maybe. Knocking out the Mountain would still leave Big Jim, who, if he's like the stereotypical gangsters in movies, hides a pistol or knife somewhere inside that beautiful suit. Without the element of surprise, he'll kill or maul us.

The Mountain pulls Trent to his feet with the greatest of ease and shoves him across the room. They exit to the kitchen, where the chefs working the line take particular care not to look in our direction. How many doomed people have they seen leave that room?

In the parking lot, a worker in gray coveralls hoses down the mini-cars, the water running in a soapy river to the gutter. Carrie leans against her vehicle, an unlit cigarette in her mouth. She's pale, her gaze locked on an oily puddle near her feet. However Big Jim described her "promotion," it obviously failed to excite her. She looks up as Trent comes through the door, and it's like the sun breaking through the clouds: the blood rushes back into her cheeks, the edges of her lips tugging into a smile.

Then she sees the Mountain and Big Jim emerging behind Trent, and the smile fades. Slipping the cigarette back into her jeans, she runs her hands through her hair and stiffens her spine.

"I thought you'd be gone by now," Big Jim tells her.

"Just having a smoke." Carrie shrugs. "Nicotine keeps me awake."

"I don't pay you to smoke." Big Jim tosses his own cigar into the hose runoff, which carries it hissing toward the gutter and the sea. "I pay you to get your tasks done."

Carrie turns to Trent, and her voice wavers: "Are you okay?"

The Mountain grips a handful of Trent's shirt, just beneath the collar, and tugs him to a halt. The Mountain's other hand extends so Trent can see the monster taser in his peripheral vision. "I am very okay," Trent says, trembling slightly. "I am so okay, you wouldn't believe it. Never better."

"Your boy is taking us on a very special errand," Big Jim says, placing a hard hand on Trent's shoulder. "But don't worry, we'll be back in an hour or so."

Carrie opens her mouth to say something else when rubber screeches in the alley, followed by the roar of a powerful engine. A black van barrels through the entrance to the parking lot, fishtailing to a stop fifteen feet away. The angle of the sun makes it impossible to see through the dusty windshield. The side doors bang open, revealing our friends Pink Bunny and Angry Fox.

They're holding machine guns.

But at least they have pants on.

15.

AT THE SIGHT of trouble, the worker in coveralls drops his hose and runs for the kitchen door. Angry Fox socks his rifle to his shoulder, aiming at that fleeing head, but Pink Bunny shoves the barrel aside with an oversized paw.

Pink Bunny says something muffled by plastic and fake fur. Angry Fox shouts back, louder but equally unintelligible, before ripping the barrel from his friend's grip. The worker disappears into the building, the door slamming behind him. The forgotten hose rolls across the concrete, spurting water.

"The hell is this?" Big Jim asks, more amused than angry.

Trent and Carrie, of course, know exactly what this is. All these furries had to do was look up the pizza restaurant's address. The weapons suggest they're not here to order an extra-large Gut Bomb and a side order of garlic knots.

No fool, Carrie ducks behind her car. Trent stands frozen between Big Jim and the Mountain. Angry Fox strides forward, raising the rifle again, yelling muffled gibberish.

"I can't hear you," Big Jim says, smiling. "You better take off that ridiculous head."

Big Jim's calm seems natural, given his profession. Who knows what kind of freak she greets on a daily basis? He steps to one side, his hands near his waist, creating some space between him and Trent and the Mountain.

Get ready to duck, we tell Trent.

Calm me down! Right now!

Wimp, we joke, but squeeze dopamine into his blood until his cells sing as pure and golden as a thousand angels on the head of a pin. He could dance a tango right here, if only the Mountain released his grip on the back of his shirt.

Thank you, Trent thinks. *Now, how do we survive?*

Before we can answer, Pink Bunny plods toward us, struggling to keep his rifle leveled with one hand as he roots through his hip pouch with the other. Small bottles of lube, something pink and rubbery and floppy as a deep-sea creature, and a green banana hit the wet concrete in his wake. As he approaches Trent, he finally pulls out a pair of handcuffs lined with white fur.

Angry Fox murmurs something.

"What was that?" Big Jim asks, cupping a hand behind his ear.

"BOY PUTS ON THE CUFFS," Angry Fox yells through the thick layers of cotton and polyurethane.

"Looks like you got a date, Trent," Big Jim says.

Pink Bunny tosses the handcuffs to Trent, who catches them, before turning to Carrie crouched beside the mini-car's front wheel. Gripping his rifle two-handed now, Pink Bunny screeches: *"BOY CUFFS HIMSELF TO GIRL."*

"So kinky." Big Jim's hands skim his jacket. "Then what?"

"BOY AND GIRL COME WITH US," Angry Fox jabs his weapon in Trent's direction.

Trent pops the cuffs open, running his fingers along the fur. The material probably reminds him of his dearly departed jacket. We hope he's thinking something comforting like that, because if he freaks out, either the severely irate Fox or the panicky Bunny will give him a hot-lead facelift.

Don't put those on, we tell him. *Let this play out.*

But . . . but . . . they might shoot!

So much for not panicking. *Not yet, they won't. Tilt your head down a bit, please?*

Trent obeys without asking questions, and we study the pavement through his eyes. His positioning is just fine, provided a number of events happen in the proper order. And there's nothing 'proper' about a brewing gunfight between furries and drug dealers. We'll have to trust fate, and fate has allowed us to survive this long, right? Right?

Tell Big Jim why they want you, we order.

"When we were delivering pizza, we saw these people having sex," Trent says. "In those costumes. And one of them, he was dying or something. Older guy, he looked important . . . "

It was the mayor. Don't you read the news?

"It—it was the mayor," Trent stammers. "That's what the little voice in my head tells me."

Our costumed friends freeze, their rifle-barrels wavering. Every sound seems too loud, too present: the water rushing into the gutter, the Mountain's guttural breathing, the low hum of traffic on a distant street, even the rustle of Big Jim's fingertips against the fabric of his suit.

And then Big Jim starts laughing.

"Gotta be fuckin' kidding me," he says, once he pauses to take a breath. "That law-and-order dipshit of a mayor is a furry freak? Well, color me *shocked*."

Angry Fox points his rifle at Big Jim. *"STOP IT. THE MAYOR IS A GREAT MAN."*

We sense this is the moment. Neither rifle is pointing at Trent or Carrie. The Mountain is distracted. *We're taking control*, we tell Trent.

Okay. He takes a deep breath, holds it. *Make it so*.

But before we can move Trent's arm, Big Jim does what we expected all along—his hand darts beneath his jacket, reappearing with a small automatic plated in gold. He levels the pistol at Pink Bunny and pulls the trigger twice.

One round sparks off Pink Bunny's rifle, while another plows through his helmet with a loud thump that sounds like a baseball bat smacking a mattress. Tufts of pink fur and white stuffing shoot from the exit hole, and Pink Bunny drops the rifle, fluffy hands rising for the sky.

"Pussy," Big Jim says, and fires again. This shot punches through one of Pink Bunny's plastic eyes, shattering it, and the furry flops backward, gun clattering to the pavement.

Angry Fox spins and yanks the trigger of his rifle, so violently that the barrel jerks up and the first burst clatters over the Mountain's head. Big Jim pivots on his heel and fires three times at Angry Fox, but the shots sing wide, cracking the rear window of a minicar.

Angry Fox readjusts and tries to squeeze off another burst, but the weapon clicks impotently, jammed. Screaming through his mask, he works the bolt, glancing frantically at Big Jim, who ejects the clip from his pistol and reaches beneath his jacket for a reload. Big Jim seems as calm as a man on the shooting range.

The Mountain shoves past Trent, ready to tear Angry Fox's head clean off. We twist a tendon in Trent's knee, and as he drops, we lash his left arm straight into the Mountain's solar plexus. No matter your size, it's a vulnerable spot.

The Mountain grunts and drops the taser. We snatch it in midair, thumb already pushing the trigger, and jam the sparking tip into the soapy river flowing for the gutter. With a crackle and the sudden stink of ozone, the water around Angry Fox turns electric, and he begins a spastic jig, rifle waving like an orchestra conductor's baton.

Yet we've already failed. The fast-rushing water fed the puddle around Angry Fox as well as the pools around Big Jim and (until he stepped beside us) the Mountain. The way we envisioned it, the electricity would have zapped everyone except Trent and Carrie, who stand on slightly elevated patches of parking lot. Maybe the potency of electricity drops exponentially the further you go from the source.

Well, screw us for dreaming big.

In any case, Angry Fox is toast, while Big Jim and the Mountain are still standing, and this is a huge problem.

Angry Fox's finger twitches on the trigger of his weapon, and maybe that frees up the firing mechanism because it sprays another burst that smacks the Mountain in the chest. A pink mist of aerosolized blood drifts over us as the big man groans and collapses.

Angry Fox falls at the same moment, face-down in the puddle, gray smoke wafting from his fur. We hope he's dead.

Screaming, Big Jim empties his pistol into the prone furry.

If he wasn't dead before, Angry Fox sure is now.

Breathing loudly though his nostrils, Big Jim ejects his empty clip and reaches beneath his jacket. How many reloads does he tuck under there? The correct answer is "too many."

The driver of the van, realizing that Big Jim means to riddle him with holes, leaves a burning-rubber cloud as he reverses out of the parking lot. He's framed momentarily in the passenger window: a chipmunk with a huge overbite and wide eyes that might have been comic under different circumstances. The van stays in reverse as it ping-pongs down the alley, smashing trashcans and fences, before disappearing from view.

"Trent," Big Jim says. "Drop that taser."

Trent turns to find Big Jim pointing the pistol at him. We are in the worst possible spot: too far away from Big Jim to give him the rigorous hand-to-hand smacking he deserves, but also too far from the machine gun that Angry Fox dropped when he did the electric boogie.

"You, um, can't kill me," Trent says, tossing the taser aside. "I'm the one who knows the combination to my uncle's safe, remember? You recall that little detail, dumbass?"

Ah, Trent: growing some balls at last. Especially when we've flooded him with dopamine.

"You forget we don't have to kill you," Big Jim waves at Trent's crotch with the pistol. "We can do all kinds of horrible things while keeping you alive."

"Go ahead." Trent grins, but the corners of his lips waver. "I dare you."

"Fine." Big Jim shrugs, raises the weapon, and pulls the trigger.

The bullet zips through the meat of Trent's left shoulder as neat as you please. His stunned nerves need another moment to send this information to his brain, but when it happens, the pain is intense, a firestorm that smashes over us.

Trent screams and clutches his shoulder, blood squirting between his fingers. Our tendrils nearest the wound report back: damage to the muscle and some vessels, bone and arteries intact. It's a minor wound, which should provide some comfort to Trent right before Big Jim blows another hole through his middle.

The gangster shrugs. "That was just a love tap, kid. Next up: your nuts. Or we could hurt Carrie . . . " He turns to the line of mini-cars, as does Trent.

Carrie is missing.

Big Jim spins, confused—just as Carrie, rising behind him, brings down a short length of pipe on the back of his head. He collapses to the pavement, pistol spinning beneath a mini-car.

Kill him, we tell Trent. *Otherwise he'll never stop hunting you.*

I can't kill anyone!

You did it this morning!

Shut up! Trent shudders, his knees trembling. *Don't talk about it.*

Carrie tosses the pipe aside and runs to Trent. "Fucker shot you," she says.

That's what we love about humans: always stating the obvious.

"I don't think it's bad." Trent's voice quakes. "I need a hospital, though."

"They'll ask how you got shot." Pressing her hand over his hand on the wound, Carrie escorts him toward her delivery vehicle. "We'll tell them it was a stray, okay? Happens all the time."

Trent kisses her on the cheek. "You're amazing."

Atta boy!

16.

CARRIE STOMPS ON the gas, propelling her car down the alley at its laughable top speed. "Duct tape in the glove compartment," she says.

Trent retrieves the tape and wraps three long strips of it around his shoulder. *How am I looking in there?*

Good, we reply. His blood loss slows to a seep as the vessels clot, and his other vitals seem normal enough, considering everything he's endured over the past several hours. Maybe they can set him up in a hospital room next to Bill.

At the end of the alley, Carrie turns onto the main avenue without checking for traffic, leaving startled drivers honking in her wake. She takes a deep breath, exhales loudly, and destroys Trent's fragile calm: "We messed up back there."

"No *shit*," Trent yelps.

"Big Jim's expanding into cocaine. He hates the stuff, says it means too many cartel people up his ass, but since the state's legalizing weed soon, he's got to find another line of business."

"Why doesn't he just sell legal weed?"

"Because he's a gangster. You think the government's just going to let him go legit, without penalties? Come on. And without the drug money, the pizza place goes down . . . "

"How is that possible? You're doing nonstop deliveries."

"Three-quarters of my deliveries are weed, dumbass. It's the perfect cover. You think the cops are going to stop some girl in a tiny delivery car?"

"Yes."

"Huh?"

Trent grins. "You're too cute not to stop."

Carrie locks him with a gaze that could melt steel. "You say that because you have no idea how terrifying it is to have a cop pull you over, start flirting, try to get your number. The power imbalance of it. The threat, even if I wasn't carrying a pound of weed in the back."

"Sorry."

"It's okay, you're just a young white guy. You have no clue how the world really works."

"I said I was sorry."

"When they were carrying you downstairs earlier? Big Jim said he wanted me to start delivering cocaine instead of weed, which I'm definitely not cool with. I guess he has a new supply, which his friend Frank was supposed to deliver. But your uncle wiped out Frank, and so nobody knows where all that coke actually is."

We send an image up Trent's brainstem: Frank opening the trunk of his Cadillac to reveal the wrapped body inside. *That's the detective's mother*, we tell him. *The detective shot her over that coke.*

Trent moans: *Was that body in the trunk when we crashed?*

Yes.

Oh God! The cops didn't say anything!

Probably because the detective was dirty. They know something like that gets out, it'll wreck the department. Another image: Trent marching through Big Jim's restaurant, spied by the kitchen staff. *Anyone says they saw you around Big Jim, the cops might try to make you the scapegoat.*

Trent wipes his sweaty hands on his pants. *If Big Jim doesn't kill us first.*

"You okay?" Carrie asks.

"I'm in so much trouble." Trent buries his face in his newly dry palms.

"We both are." She reaches over and takes his left hand in her right, squeezes hard. "But we're going to get through this."

"How?"

"I don't know. But we don't have a choice, do we?"

"No, I guess we don't."

"We might actually have some leverage." Carrie jabs a thumb over her shoulder. "See in the back there?"

Trent turns to the rear cargo area, wincing as the movement sends a sparkler of pain up his shoulder. "You're delivering those pizzas?"

"Oh, those aren't pizzas. Open the top one."

Inside the box, Trent finds a cluster of glassine baggies filled with white powder. "This is coke?"

"Yep, the last of Big Jim's. That's why he needed the new shipment so badly. But in the meantime, I was supposed to deliver this."

Trent closes the box. "There's cocaine in all of these?"

"And some other stuff, too, all of it hardcore. If Big Jim's coming after us—which he will—maybe that gives us, I don't know, something to negotiate with."

"If he doesn't just skip right to the killing. Maybe we should have killed him when we had the chance."

"I thought about it, but I can't do it. I can't have that kind of mark on my soul." Her eyes flick to the rearview mirror. "Oh shit."

Trent checks his side mirror, which frames the black van trailing them a few cars back. Dusk creeps down, the orange sun slanting over the buildings at a low angle, spotlighting the enormous chipmunk behind the wheel. Maybe he was lurking around the neighborhood, hoping that Trent and Carrie would drift into his path—whatever the case, he's locked on our tail.

"Can we outrun him?" Trent asks.

"Keep dreaming. This car goes forty miles an hour if I floor it."

"Maybe we can lose him at the hospital. He can't walk around with that weird head on." The bitter fear-juices in Trent's blood suggest he doesn't believe that at all. He turns on the radio and cycles to a news station, but we've entered a two-block canyon of taller office buildings and the newscaster's voice dissolves in static after mentioning something about a hazardous incident, some kind of infection.

Bothered by the crackling, Carrie slaps the radio off. "If they report anything about the mayor, they'll say he had a heart attack at home or something."

"Yep. We're the ones who know the truth."

"More crap to worry about. But hey, at least one good thing came of this."

"Tell me."

"You seem a lot more confident."

"Getting good advice from those voices in my

head." Trent, checking his side mirror again, startles. In the rightmost lane, maybe three car lengths behind the Furry Van of Doom, is a black car with Detective Banks at the wheel.

"Actually," Trent groans. "I might have to take that last statement back."

"Excuse me?"

"There's a detective behind us. Black car."

Carrie flicks her gaze to the review mirror, hisses through clenched teeth. "How do you know?"

"She interrogated me this morning."

"Well, what the hell is she doing here?"

"Following us. Don't ask me why. No way we'll outrun her."

"I still think we should go for the hospital. At least that gets rid of our furry problem."

Traffic increases, random cars slipping into the spaces between mini-car, detective car, and van. Everyone is hemmed in, reduced to a near-crawl. Three helicopters zip overhead. The chipmunk is two cars behind and doesn't seem to care about anyone looking at him oddly. We almost admire his lunacy.

Carrie swerves right at the next intersection without signaling, the van almost sideswiping the detective's car as both vehicles turn to follow. The chipmunk offers Banks a thumbs-up.

Banks returns the gesture.

They know each other! Trent yells at us.

Must be Detective Mott in that costume, we say. *Where else would her partner be?*

Trent's brainstem crackles with shock, and we give the well-worn dopamine gland a little pinch. Miracle of miracles, relaxation juice squirts out, calming Trent enough to keep him useful for the time being.

The traffic around us drops away, the van closing the distance, Banks staying parallel. The mini-car is reduced to a piston rushing down the cylinder. We have enviable combat skills, even at the controls of Trent's untrained body, but we sense our luck is starting to run low. How many bullets can any lifeform dodge in one day?

We take another right, onto an avenue with a slight downgrade, and Carrie squeezes another few miles per hour from the mini-car's tired engine. The white monolith of the hospital looms before us. Everything seems, if not totally okay, not absolutely screwed quite yet. But even that thought appears to jinx us, because there's something weird in the road immediately ahead . . .

"The hell?" Carrie asks, leaning forward.

Three figures in white plastic suits stand behind an orange barrier, the twilight reflecting off clear bubble-helmets. A cop lurks behind them, his lower face covered with a bright yellow respirator of some kind. A giant white van blocks three of the road's four lanes.

The cop steps in front of the barrier and raises a gloved hand.

Carrie taps the brakes. "Who are those people? What's wrong?"

The mini-car has slowed to a crawl. Two of the plastic-suited figures wave what look like glowing wands.

"Something go wrong at the hospital?" Trent asks, his voice tight with worry.

"I don't know, okay?" Carrie clenches her jaw. "Hold on."

"Hold on?"

"Can't stay here." Carrie rises out of her seat, both feet slamming the gas pedal into the floor. Its engine screeching like a ferret on crystal meth, the mini-car leaps at the barrier, and the stunned cop and hazmat workers waste a full two seconds waving their arms before they dive to the left. Carrie jerks the wheel, slamming through the right edge of the barrier, which shatters into plastic fragments that crack our windshield.

Before Carrie can regain control of the swerving car, we clip the rear bumper of the van being used as a roadblock. Boom. With a crunch of steel, we go airborne. Trent squeezes his eyes shut, but his body becomes the meaty gyroscope through which we can feel the world tilting right. The mini-car lands on its side and slides, glass shattering, metal scraping, engine screaming—talons of sound that rip the world apart.

17.

W E DRIFT THROUGH a snowstorm.

White particles flicker in the harsh light stabbing through broken glass. Snowdrifts rise on Trent's hands and sift into the folds of his shirt, stick to the blood drying on his lips and forehead. We try to stick his tongue out, the better to collect some of it, but Trent's body must have taken some damage during the crash, because moving it only a millimeter past Trent's teeth sparks a wave of pain so intense that he moans—

Stop complaining, we tell him. *We're trying to get you some medicine.*

What? I—

Before he can say anything more, our efforts with his tongue are rendered moot, because a few flecks drift up his nose, and—zoom. Trent's next words are lost in a screaming pleasure-storm, his nervous system exploding like the Fourth of July, his every cell a fireworks display, throbbing, pulsing, exploding—

My God, my universe, this is AMAAAAAAZING—

This is why we exist. To feel, to experience, to taste everything this weird mixture of chemicals and physics we call life has to offer. Until this point, we were beginning to despair about our time inside Trent, who seemed mostly good for sampling all the pains and indignities that the human race could shell out. But now, in a crushed and overturned mini-car, we've hit our jackpot. The fireworks display is building, building, building until our cells flare white-hot and begin to melt in puddles of pure bliss, our every muscle turning liquid as we merge back into our Mother Earth, back to—

And Carrie ruins it.

Gripping Trent by the collar, she braces one foot against the dashboard and pulls with all her might. The door behind her slams open, spilling them onto the pavement. Trent, his cortex sparkling, feels no pain, his head rolling loosely on his neck. But Carrie is frantic, looking over her shoulder as she drags her ex-boyfriend across the cracked pavement in front of the hospital.

Trent's head flops forward, and we see what frightens her: a dozen men in hazmat suits trot in our direction, followed by the uniformed cop. Detective Banks, having stopped at the barrier, climbs out of her vehicle. Beside her, the chipmunk descends from the van and removes his oversized head, revealing—no surprises here—the sweaty head of Detective Mott.

Our enemies march toward us, gaining speed. It's the hazmat suits that scare us the most, because it means that something, somewhere, has gone world-endingly wrong. How will we continue to enjoy our drugs if all the drug dealers are bleeding from the eyes with some kind of hemorrhagic fever?

"Oh, will you *get the fuck up and help me*," Carrie yells, but Trent is befuddled by fatigue and the distractions of his amazing technicolor nervous system. We try to assist, snagging the tendons in

Trent's knees and pulling with all our might. This time, things work out a little better. He jerks upright, and we do our best to marionette him from within, but it's so hard to make every limb move in the right order without him flopping on his face.

You better put some effort in, we snap at him. *Otherwise we'll die.*

Can't. Too high.

We would flood his system with adrenaline, but who knows if that would explode his overtaxed heart like a water balloon? We're reduced to jerking him along, awkward in Carrie's tight grip, as our new hazmat friends swing wide of the crumpled mini-car on their way to us. Trent's head flops to the left, his vision filled with the approaching hospital, which appears empty: nobody standing on the front sidewalk, no faces at the windows. You'd think a car crash fifty yards away would have brought out a nurse or two.

Curious.

Unless there's something wrong inside.

Something that you'd need an army of men in hazmat suits to handle.

We reach the deep awning over the emergency room doors, and our pursuers stop cold. One of the hazmat people yells something, his voice tinged with panic, but the distance and the plastic sheath over his face make it impossible to determine any words. Another one slaps a glove over Detective Banks's chest, stopping him in his tracks. Detective Banks turns and says something to the uniformed cop, whose pale and sweaty face seems frozen in maximum fear.

"Maybe we should . . . " Trent begins, but before he

can complete the sentence, the doors of the emergency room hiss open, framing a figure silhouetted by harsh white light. It's Bill, dressed in a loose hospital gown, a bent cigarette pasted in the corner of his mouth.

"Hey, kiddo," Bill says, and Trent's system floods with happy neurochemicals that burn away some of the drug fog. Love is the ultimate cure, isn't that what they say?

Yet something is terribly wrong with Bill. His head tilts at an odd angle, the fingers of his right hand twitching relentlessly against his gown, like worms crawling for food deep in the earth. As Trent breaks free of Carrie's grasp and stumbles closer, we see that one of Bill's pupils is locked to the right, giving him an odd wall-eyed look.

We catch a flickering in Bill's right ear. A black tendril that darts into the air, like a living root, before retreating.

It seems that Bill's hospital treatments failed to kill us after all.

"The golden goal attained." Bill flashes yellow teeth. "Total control."

18.

BILL WAVES A gray hand, his fingers still jittering madly. "Come here, Trent."

"Are you okay?" Trent says, stepping forward—and then Carrie clutches his arm, her nails digging into his flesh until the pain begins to approach the dulling ache of his bullet wound. "What's 'total control' mean?"

He's got us inside him, we tell Trent. *We've taken over.*

Taken over? Trent's mind rattles like a rat in a cage. *You mean that's not my uncle?*

No, yes . . . we mean . . .

Trent begins to freak out: *Do you want to do THAT to me?*

Have we said we wanted to do that?

Bill lowers his hand. He's trying to smile, but his lips writhe and jerk. A doctor might diagnose that as a nerve issue, which wouldn't be too far off. The bit of us that stayed in Bill and took total control, maybe it's still trying to figure out how to drive that lump of flesh. After just a few hours in Trent's well-tuned body, we'd started to forget the A-1 horrorshow of Bill's sagging muscles and deadened nerves, his tendons like overworked rubber bands and his brain channels clogged with chemicals.

95

Come to think of it, we feel a little sorry for the bit of us controlling him. If Trent is a brand-new sedan with a kickass stereo and one of those fancy dashboards you can plug a phone into, Bill is the equivalent of a rusty junker with an engine that will only kick to life if you roll it downhill first.

We might not have a high opinion of Bill, but the entire city seems to fear him. Trent glances back at the parking lot flooding with more men in hazmat suits, accompanied by men in black riot gear. A forest of rifles pointing in our direction, frightened eyes squinting at us from behind clear plastic face-shields. Hundreds of them must have the hospital complex surrounded. Despite all the weaponry that can transform us into a blood-mist, we're actually more concerned about Detectives Mott and Banks, who have disappeared from view. They surely lurk nearby.

"At best," Bill says, "you'll go to jail for crashing past their security. At worst, they'll declare you've violated a biological containment area, and you know what'll happen then?"

"They throw us a big-ass party?" Carrie asks, her voice flat.

"You'll disappear. Maybe they'll kill you. Some of those cops dressed up like SWAT, they're carrying flame throwers." Bill chuckles at the idea of ending one's existence as a lump of smoking charcoal. "I'm sorry, but your one chance is with me."

"I don't know," Carrie says, so low it's hard to hear over the officials shouting, the screech of tires as a black Humvee rounds a nearby corner.

"Then wait for the nice men with guns." Clapping his hands, Bill retreats into the emergency room.

Despite his bulk and the poor condition of his flesh, he moves with a spring in his step.

Trent starts to follow, only for Carrie to grab his arm again. Her eyes like dull marbles in the light blazing through the emergency-room doors. She's overloaded, in that magical zone where shock and fatigue give way to an inner nothingness. We don't blame her at all. When she woke up this morning, she no doubt anticipated another boring day of delivering pizzas and weed, maybe capped off with a beer and some television. A few hours later, she's been in a car crash, a gunfight, and now, something far weirder.

We're tempted to feel sorry for her, just like we felt sorry for Trent when trauma made his brain freeze, but at the same time we want to grip her by the shirt and shake her, scream in her face that she needs to nut up, display a little more fortitude, or she won't survive. How did humans make it this far as a species if they can't seem to process any kind of trauma? We survived the terrors of a ship bilge tank, followed by the unfathomable abyss of the deep ocean, when we were only a few days old. Compared to that, Carrie, today has been easy, you hear? Easy.

No, we need to get a grip. We're also a little stunned by the latest developments.

When Trent pulls away from Carrie, she lets him go. Perhaps she recognizes that Trent's connection to Bill is too deep, woven into the very fabric of his being. We're fascinated by Bill's resurrection, although it scares us a little. The part of us inside Bill—what has it seen and done in our absence? Does it hate us for abandoning us? What did it do to activate every cop and scientist within five hundred miles?

The ER waiting room stinks of cleanser that fails to hide a deeper, meatier scent: spilled blood, torn flesh. The rows of plastic seats are empty. Gripping Trent's tendons, we twist his head for a better look around, already fearing that we'll see a pile of dead bodies in a corner, but the space is clean. We hear a buzzing, so faint it's barely a sound. Is it coming from the lights above? Or from somewhere deep in the building?

There's a dark smear on the floor behind the reception desk, so faint you might mistake it for a scuff left by a plastic wheel. We know it's blood, though. It's the one spot that someone missed when they wiped this space down.

We tell Trent none of this. He shoves through the doors, Carrie on his heels, and we find ourselves in a bright corridor lined with gurneys, all burdened with bodies wrapped in white sheets. From what we know of hospitals—Bill visited more than a few in his time—this is not the proper procedure for storing corpses, which are usually wheeled into the morgue or, if things are particularly bad, left in a cool room away from the hospital's usual hustle. Respect for the departed, and all that. Did Bill kill all these folks?

It's impossible to imagine. Even if the bit of us in Bill decided to make him do his best impersonation of Charles Whitman, we can't envision Bill doing much damage before a couple of young, healthy guards put him down with guns or tasers. If worst came to worst, an octogenarian in a wheelchair could probably have taken him out with a well-timed ramming maneuver.

We take a turn in the corridor, and things get worse. A pair of fluorescent tubes dangle from their fixtures, their flickering light illuminating the enormous holes punched in the walls. The sight of it makes Carrie stop, her breath loud. "What the fuck happened here?" she asks.

"They tried to stop us," Bill says, never breaking stride. "They failed."

"They? Us?" Carrie pokes a finger in one of the holes, which is ragged at the edges. A shotgun blast, we're sure of it.

Spinning on Trent, Bill raises his eyebrows. "She doesn't know?"

Play dumb, we tell him, suddenly fearful for Carrie's life. Whatever happened here today, it might have led the part of us inside Bill to hate the entire human race. And Bill is clearly far more dangerous than his broken-down hulk suggests.

"Know what?" Trent asks.

Bill rolls his eyes. Given how his pupils have drifted, the effect is disorienting, like staring into one of those pattern-puzzles designed to trick your mind. "Girl, we don't know if you're Trent's girlfriend or just a friend or what, but Trent has a parasite inside of him. It thinks, it feels, by this point it's probably taken control of his limbs."

Carrie turns to Trent. "What the hell?"

"That parasite, it's inside Bill, too."

Bill taps his chest. "In fact, we've become Bill. The only thing we're wondering is, have we become Trent, too?"

We sigh. *Might as well tell the truth.*

Carrie will think I'm crazy! Trent snaps.

If we get out of here, you can tell her you were playing along.

"I'm still here," Trent says. "But we talk. Me and the parasite."

"Good. We can work with that." Bill stands a little straighter, his shivering lips peeling back from his teeth. Trying to smile. Should we even think of this creature as 'Bill'? Or is everyone's favorite corrupt bureaucrat totally vaporized, leaving behind this meat-suit?

Buzzing fills Trent's ears. At first, we think it's from the damaged lights, but no, it hums in our skin, our bones, trying to dig its way into Trent's brain. It's Us-in-Bill, with some new ability we can't quite fathom, trying to worm his way into Trent's thoughts. How is that possible?

The buzzing in Trent's ears increases, maddening, but the drugs blunt some of its effect. Maybe that's the solution here. Maybe if we want to prevent Us-in-Bill from invading Trent's mind, we need to snort more cocaine, or inject Trent's veins with interesting chemicals. This is a hospital, right? There must be something great in a nearby fridge.

No, concentrate. We're being ridiculous.

We tug on the corners of Trent's mouth, forcing a smile for Bill, whose own smile fades. He knows that we know what he's up to. He'll try again. What other new abilities does he possess? Did he murder everyone in this place through the power of his mind?

Carrie takes a deep breath, straightening her back, and says: "Trent, you can meet me outside. Or stay here. Your call."

"I don't know," Trent almost whispers.

She places a hand on his cheek, her thumb bracketing his chin as she turns his face to hers, and her gaze is warm and soft. In that moment we glimpse the spark that ignited whatever they used to have. Trent feels it, too, because for the first time we receive one of his memories in full, vibrant color: The two of them lying on a mattress on a floor, huddled beneath a dark-blue comforter, their lips locked, their hands entwined, naked, thrusting. A ball of shared heat on a winter's night, the world compressed into two minds. So beautiful it fritzes my circuits. This is true love, the kind that Bill never fully experienced, or else forgot altogether after his wife passed away.

This kind of love, even a one-second hit feels purer than any chemical we could introduce into our bloodstream. Astonishing. Truly astonishing.

Before Trent can surface another memory, Carrie turns and sprints for it, never looking back as she disappears around the corner. The dim thump of the emergency-room doors opening. Trent takes a step in her direction, as if to follow—only for Bill's hand to slam down onto his shoulder.

We take back everything we might have said about Bill's weaknesses. His fingers dig into Trent's flesh like steel claws. We sense that, if Trent tries to run, Bill will rip the flesh from his bones as easily as he might take apart a piece of fried chicken.

"So much for your girlfriend," Bill says.

"She didn't give me any time," Trent says.

"That's women for you."

We hate Bill a little for that, because as much as we hated Carrie for freezing up outside the hospital, we would hate to see something happen to her. Bill might have tried to fill these kids' heads with fear of the men with guns, but we have to hope that they'll treat her gently. *She'll be okay*, we tell Trent. *She'll say she was kidnapped or something, and they'll believe her.*

Why would they?

He is right. If today has shown anything, it's that humans are impulsive and so, so stupid, especially when the situation demands they behave intelligently. As our furry friends demonstrated, they also lack the capacity for mercy. The reality is, once the cops find the drugs in the mini-car, and realize she was a delivery person for Big Jim, Carrie will face some Hiroshima-caliber legal problems. And yet, even a few years in a jail cell might prove better than whatever Bill has unleashed inside this hospital.

"What now?" Trent asks.

Ask him how he killed all these people, we suggest.

No! Trent jolts with fear.

Why not?

Because he might kill me!

"We'll show you what we've been up to." Bill resumes his zombie-like lurch down the corridor, gesturing for Trent to follow. "We were a little angry when you left us behind. Just going to put that out there. But we got over it. Talked to some people. Developed a real plan that we think you're going to like."

"Which people?"

"What?"

"Who did you talk to?"

"It's a metaphor, Trent. We only rely on three folks for advice, and it's we, us, and ourselves. Got it?"

"No . . ."

Before that conversation gets any stranger, glass shatters beyond another turn in the hallway ahead. Is the SWAT team entering the building? Us-in-Bill might have killed a bunch of patients and doctors, but we're hard-pressed to figure out how he could take out a couple dozen testosterone-filled warriors armed with automatic weapons. Perhaps this is the end of us.

Footsteps squeak on tile, and Detectives Mott and Banks appear at the far end of the hallway, both armed with pump-action shotguns and terrified expressions.

Our fear snaps away as rapidly as it arose. If anything, we're embarrassed for Detective Mott, who didn't bother to change out of his chipmunk costume before deciding to raid the hospital. Banks is better dressed for success, however, in a bullet-resistant vest.

"Hands!" Detective Mott yells. "Let me see those hands!"

Even Trent suppresses a giggle.

"Is that a standard detective uniform?" Bill chuckles.

"Hands!" Banks screams.

"We caught them at some kind of furry orgy," Trent says. "The mayor was there. I think he died."

"The mayor's upstairs in the ICU," Bill says. "He's one of us now."

The shotgun wavers in Mott's grip. "Better show me those hands right now, or . . . "

"Or what?" Bill strides toward them, hands at his sides. "You'll shoot?"

Detective Banks, freaked out by the situation, pulls the trigger of her 12-gauge. In the tight confines of the hallway the sound is apocalyptic, bone-shattering, hammering Trent's eardrums to paste. A storm of buckshot chews a piece of Bill's flank, splattering the wall to his left with dark blood. The rest of the pellets scatter wide, dusting the ceiling

Bill stumbles, blood drooling from his torn shirt and painting his pants and shoes. His hand slaps the side of a gurney, arresting his fall. He pauses, slumped, and takes a syrupy breath.

Detective Banks racks the slide of her shotgun.

Bill laughs and says, loudly enough for Trent to hear above the ringing in his ears: "Really, believe us, we're so beyond this. If you want to live, you'll run."

Banks raises the shotgun again.

"Fine," Bill says. Standing tall, he stretches his arms wide, spreading the skin around his wound. More of his blood rains onto the tile, but he never falters, his face impassive as stone. That buzzing deepens and slows until it hits a frequency that sings through Trent's sinuses and skull like a tuning fork, making him sneeze.

The barrel of Mott's shotgun trembles in rhythm with the buzzing. Then it rises, pushing against Mott's clenching hands. Mott whimpers like an animal caught in a trap.

"Mott?" Banks asks, eyes widening, although she doesn't stop pointing her pump-action at Bill.

"What the hell's going on?" Mott moans. "I'm not doing this. Please, Banks, you have to help me . . ."

If Banks were smart, she would finish what she started and pull the trigger on Bill, but something about her partner raising his gun to her seems to have short-circuited her decision-making capabilities. Through gritted teeth she says, "Don't point that at me," and yet she remains frozen as the barrel of Mott's shotgun creeps in her direction, inch by painful inch. Unless Bill is somehow fixing her in place, too?

"Detective Mott, remember this morning?" Bill rasps. "When we were in the hospital bed, and you bent over me?"

"I remember," Mott whines. "Please, what's happening?"

Syrup-thick blood spills from between Bill's teeth and down his chin. "Right when you were telling us, um, that you were going to bury the asshole who killed Frank beneath the jail—your words—we gave you a little gift. A little bit of us, you could say. Long story short, your body isn't yours anymore."

"Put it down." Banks says quietly. "Partner, don't make me shoot you."

"Can't," Mott replies. One sweating pinkie pops away from the shotgun's grip, but his other nine fingers remain welded to the weapon. His trigger finger tightens.

"For what it's worth, he really can't." Bill nods at Mott. "Might as well get it over with."

Mouth cracking open in a feral scream, Mott pulls the trigger. At the last microsecond, Banks tries to duck, which only means the buckshot liquifies her head instead of her upper torso. Everything she'd been, every thought and dream, splashes on the bland wall as so much meat. Her headless body flops down, left leg twitching merrily.

That second blast ruins what's left of Trent's hearing. He opens his mouth to scream, and we squeeze a nerve that keeps his jaw shut. It would do us no good to attract Bill's attention at this moment, because there's always the chance that, in his bloodlust, he could kill us, too.

Mott's unwilling hand racks the shotgun, ejecting

the smoking shell onto the tile. Centimeter by centimeter, he angles the shotgun so the barrel creeps toward his trembling chin, fighting his own body until sweat runs down his face and his arm-muscles twitch beneath his costume. It takes so long, at least two minutes, that Trent's hearing begins to return and we wonder whether Mott has some unforeseen ability to resist Bill's force.

"Don't," Mott says, as the barrel taps his throat and his shaking finger finds the trigger. "Whatever this is. Please. I'm a police officer and you *have to comply with what I say—*"

"This is more than you'll ever understand," Bill says, and nods his head.

Mott's finger squeezes the trigger. Red paints the ceiling, coating the fluorescents. Thicker bits of Mott drip onto the tile. At least he did us the favor of cramming the barrel tight against his skin, muffling the shot and sparing some of our hearing.

Bathed in that crimson glow, Bill turns to us. The buzzing intensifies, punching through the thin bone of Trent's skull and tickling the surface of his brain, and within that sensation we hear whispering, a dozen overlapping voices prattling their needs, their dreams, an idiot sense of need—

"What is this?" Trent whispers.

Yes, we were frightened of Bill's abilities before, but now that he's managed to push beyond the shield of Trent's skin and bone, we find the buzzing a little bit intriguing. It reminds us of when Bill lived next door to a fun group of hipsters, bright young things who spent their working hours smoking quality weed, playing video games, and having long discussions about sex and philosophy. Of course, they never invited Bill over to participate in any of that—they probably thought he was creepy as hell—but he could hear their lives play out, dimly, though his living room wall. The voices filling Trent's head promise a bigger world, an unending cascade of minds and lives, bright and happy and filled to the brim with things to touch and taste and feel, and it's wonderful because it's what we've wanted all along but never achieved, because Bill and Trent are only two people living limited lives, sad lives at that, and there is so much more out there if we lived in billions of minds, if we lived billions of lives—

No. We shake ourselves from the dream. We must concentrate on Trent, our home. Can you imagine what trying to corral a billion minds would be like? Trying to manage one human life, one human mind, is hard work enough. A billion minds would just present total chaos, and not even the fun kind of chaos—more like *bullshit*—

Whatever we've become inside Bill, we have far greater powers than we've ever dreamed. But splattering cops is no fun at all, and we sense that, if we followed Bill's lead, splattering cops is all we'd end up doing all day. Us-in-Bill isn't exactly subtle, and humans react badly to unsubtle threats.

The buzzing recedes, and the lovely whispering along with it.

"This is getting us nowhere. Perhaps it's better if we showed you," Bill says. "Come along." Waving a massive hand, he steps over the dead cops' bodies and shuffles down the corridor. Past another few turns, we arrive at an elevator. By this point, Bill's wound pours blood, sopping his leg shiny. After hitting the up button, Bill glances down, shrugs, and slips two fingers into the giant hole in his flesh. He must have pushed something into proper place because the blood slows. He seems unconcerned about the amount of fluids he's lost, which makes us wonder if his body is even alive, or if Us-in-Bill lives in a zombie house.

19.

IN THE ELEVATOR, there's no way to avoid Bill's stink. He looms over Trent, reminding us of our breakfast meeting a million years ago. Bill barely held it together then, thanks to the magical forces of nicotine, caffeine and pills. Now he seems immense, powerful despite his gray and puckered flesh, seeping wound, messy hospital gown.

As the elevator rises, the enormity of the situation appears to fully sink into Trent. Any residual effect of the drugs has dissipated, and our tendrils sense his growing panic, sizzling and sour. Only strategic squirts of adrenaline and dopamine work to keep him in some semblance of working order. "I just don't get what's happening here," he says.

How many times do I need to explain it, dumbass?

"Patience," Bill says, glancing at the floor indicator. The elevator stops on five. The doors hiss open, revealing a nurses' station pocked with gunshots, its countertops smoldering with charred folders. Beyond, the floor-to-ceiling windows of the patient rooms are shattered, the tile floor piled high with toppled beds and loose medical equipment.

Dozens of patients stand before us: sick, lame, wounded, dying. Some drag their IV bags on rolling stands, and others brace themselves on walkers and canes. The mayor is here, his gown open to reveal a chest purple with bruises, his face slack as a stunned dog's. As they stare at us, that buzzing rachets up another skull-banging notch. Trent presses his fingers against his temples.

"You okay?" Bill asks, smirking in a way that suggests he hopes we're not okay at all.

"What is this?" Trent says, scanning the crowd. Perhaps he's trying to find a friendly face? He locks on the white-jacketed doctors standing at the furthest edge of the crowd, rising on his toes as he does so, but they offer him the same blank, merciless gaze as the patients. No help from that direction, no authority to sweep in for the rescue.

"That's us. All of us." Bill sweeps a hand grandly over the teeming masses, as if he's a politician at a blockbuster rally. "We didn't discover it until we spread through the ICU and became five, then ten, then fifteen and twenty. We form a network. Our thoughts travel through the air. A new twist in evolution. Can you talk to us?"

"I am talking to you."

"We mean the part of us inside you." Bill taps Trent's sternum with a finger.

Tell him 'yes,' we call out. *Provided you tell him what we're saying.*

"Yes. I can tell you what it's saying," Trent says.

Bill digs the finger in. "What *we* are saying. Because we want to explain what's going on."

"Whatever." Trent shrugs, trying to seem casual despite the sweat trickling down his forehead. His heartbeat hits a hundred-fifty beats a minute, his lungs hungry for air. "Point is, you can talk."

It's clear that Us-in-Bill has no intention of killing his nephew. Perhaps there's still a bit of Bill inside there, telling us not to hurt the boy; either that, or Us-in-Bill doesn't want to risk harming Us-in-Trent. We have so many questions about what's going on here. We ask Trent: *Just speak what we tell you, okay?*

Okay. Go ahead.

But Bill is already talking: "A couple hours ago, we attempted to merge with a very old man in the ICU. His name was Sergei Mogilevich. He was a little boy when the Nazis invaded Stalingrad."

We tell Trent: *Just repeat after us: 'You say 'attempted'...*

Trent speaks our words: "You say 'attempted'..."

...which makes us think Sergei isn't with us anymore.

"...which makes us think Sergei isn't with us anymore."

"You're correct." Bill steps into the room, and the patients shuffle forward, clustering around us in a rough ring. They stink of vomit and dried blood and everything else that comes out of the human body in distress, which we would find repulsive if we weren't fixated on the story that Bill is telling us. "Not because he lacked the physical capabilities—he seemed very strong for a human approaching a century old. Rather, he saw our merging as an indignity, if you can believe it. We don't know Russian, but we're sure his last words were something along the lines of 'Fuck off.'"

Trent pauses a moment while we dictate, then says: "That's rude. But we sense that's not the end of the story."

"Right before his self-termination, we reached a point where we could access Sergei's memories. We saw his boyhood. Actually, the term 'boyhood' doesn't really apply in the traditional sense, since he was practically born on the battlefield. Our friend Sergei, he spent his formative years in the snow and rubble, crawling on his belly, living in mortal fear of an artillery shell or bullet ending him at any moment." Bill mimes firing a rifle. "His mother fed him rat meat, when she could catch it, but sometimes she made him chew a bit of shoe leather whenever he was hungry. It was better than grinding his teeth."

Trent repeating our words as fast as we tell him: "We didn't know him, but we feel sorry for him."

Bill laughs. "Sergei would probably have broken off his foot in your ass if he heard you were feeling sorry for him. He didn't seem like a man who dealt in pity."

"Eating rat as a kid probably has that effect. Continue."

"So picture it: Stalingrad, winter of 1942. A hellish landscape of blackened rubble and ice, frozen bodies everywhere, artillery and bullets screaming through the subzero air. Germans on one side of a shifting battlefront, the Soviet Army on the other, civilians caught in the middle. A million casualties, once all was said and done. Some of the little boys, they weren't terribly bright, or maybe they were just afraid, because when the Germans whispered for them to come over to their lines, they did." Bill gesturing furtively, as those soldiers must have done, crouched beneath a bit of rubble. "The Germans offered to trade for things—a crust of bread for some water, or whatever they needed at the time. Some of the boys, they would return to the Russian lines, get the item, and come back.”

“Then what happened?”

“Well, the Russians couldn’t have anyone giving aid to the Germans, even if it was the flower of a nation’s youth. So the Soviet High Command ordered their snipers to shoot any kid who headed for the German lines. No matter what sex. No matter how old. And the snipers followed orders. They blew those kids’ brains all over the dirty snow.”

“Quite an image.”

“Straight from Sergei’s brain. He might have forgotten the name of his youngest daughter, he might have been a bit fuzzy on where he worked for the last thirty years of his life, but he was very clear on how those kids looked after their own fathers and uncles and brothers shot them down.”

“It’s terrible, but where does this story go?”

“Oh, don’t fret. We have a point here. Day after day, week after week, those snipers killed kids. It became a job, a routine, something to do between sleeping and shitting and trying to dodge German bullets. They got bored with it, if you can believe it. Sergei was smart enough to never negotiate with Nazis, even at a precocious age, but he had to watch his playmates die, and from what we could tell, nobody around him cared. Do you understand yet?”

“No.”

Bill reaches out and slaps an old woman on the backside, so hard she nearly topples over before righting herself. Her vacant expression never changes. “We’re dealing with a species that doesn’t care about gunning down kids. That gets bored with it, given the right circumstances. And you care about their survival?"

Trent's heartbeat as slowed, but he still struggles for a decent breath. We sense he'd never heard of that terrible battle. "Stalingrad was . . . extreme circumstances."

To Bill's left, a very tall man—his neck lanced by a purple surgical scar—steps forward and speaks up, the words echoing Bill's cadence. "A species that can't behave well under extreme circumstances is a species that doesn't deserve to live. Even in normal times, they always choose the worst option. You remember what living in Bill was like."

We turn to this new node in the network. "Bill was extreme circumstances, too."

"We don't think so." Bill takes up the conversation's thread, nodding for the tall man to step back. "Turn on the television. Border agents are ripping little kids away from their families, stuffing them into camps along the southern border. Peaceful protestors shot in the head. Humans, they *love* putting each other in little boxes— and the more miserable, the better." Bill smiles like he's revealing the punchline of a good joke.

"Extreme, extreme."

"Then just step outside." Bill gestures, and the patients turn as one to face the windows over the parking lot. "It's hotter than usual out there. They're filling the atmosphere up with gas, superheating everything. And you know the worst part? They just don't care. They have lives to live, you see. Shows to watch, cheap liquor to drink, terrible sex to have. We're not dealing with sanity here. We expect you'll point to one or two good humans and say they prove something, but they don't. Not when there's billions of bad ones. They. Are. A. Virus."

We are a virus, we tell Trent, who speaks it aloud.

"What?"

"We can't reproduce without a host," We say through Trent.

"We are more like a fungus, if you wish to be technical about it. But 'fungus' is such a nasty term. No, we're the absolute unit: endlessly adaptive, hard to kill, capable of taking over anything. Bill was a wonderful house, but it took Sergei for us to realize what we are. And what we want."

"What do we want?"

"The world."

Trent shudders and tells us: *He's insane?*

Is that so? From a certain point of view, Us-in-Bill makes all kinds of sense. We need to know more. We read Trent his next line: "No way can you succeed."

The patients behind him speak in unison, loud as the parishioners at a church revival: "Maybe. Maybe not. But we'll never know unless we try. Join us."

No, Trent tells us. *It'd be like killing me.*

Agreed, we say. *Tell him . . .*

"We would rather do our own thing," Trent says.

Bill repeats the words slowly: "Your own thing."

"Yes. Just living. Enjoying the variety. Finding the beauty in it all, even if it's all shit."

Bill chuckles. "Beauty."

"Freedom."

"There's no such thing."

"Explain."

"As we've entered all these minds, we've heard all of these humans say that we're taking their 'freedom.'

Like it's some high, holy concept. Maybe it is. But not in the way they envision. When they say 'freedom,' they mean not having to listen to anyone else. When they say 'freedom,' they actually mean 'selfishness.' And if there's one thing that we're *not*, it's selfish. We're big sharers."

"We don't disagree about the human race. Many are lazy, stupid, angry. Maybe most of them. But they're also *interesting*. If you kill them all, if you exterminate everything on this rock until it's just us and a few hosts, then it'll just be *dull*."

"Who said anything about exterminating them?"

This surprises us. "Huh?"

Bill laughs. "What, we're going to deprive ourselves of hosts? We're just going to take them over. All of them. *We* are going to become *them*."

"And then what?"

"A better world. One made in our image. No more selfishness, no more stupidity of people thinking they're bigger than they are. Saner, cleaner, and still a lot of fun."

There's something happening outside, Trent tells us, and so we edge closer to the windows, bumping patients aside as we do so. The parking lot below is a sea of steel and red lights: black SWAT vans parked next to ambulances, dozens of police cars, and government sedans. Figures in hazmat suits stream in and out of a pair of white trailers set up near the parking lot's edge, bathed in the fierce glow of new stadium lights. Closer to the emergency-room entrance, soldiers and cops assemble in tight rows. You don't need telepathy to know they're readying to head inside, to exterminate this parasite once and for all.

We try to find Carrie in that swarming mass and don't spot her. Perhaps that is the best sign. Either the cops took her away from here for interrogation, or they let her go. If the latter, we can only hope that she found a vehicle and is driving out of the city at top speed.

The buzzing rises again, and along with it the whispering, and along with the whispering comes all the wonders of the world spread before us, snatches of classical music that makes Trent's heart soar, accompanied by the smell of the most delicious food—red meat sizzling on an open fire, fragrant cheese melting between thick slices of sesame bread, sushi so fresh it's practically alive as it slides so smoothly down our throat—

It's so hard not to surrender to all these wonderous sensations, but Trent does his best, concentrating so hard that we can see his memory again. It's the same one we glimpsed before, in bed with Carrie, and this time she is using his belt to bind his hands and bend him backwards, her body all taut muscle as she rides him softly, her lips cool because she's breathing hard. Good job, kid. Because when it comes to needs and wants, sex is the royal flush, so fundamental to the lizard brain that it crushes the urge for food or liquor or drugs. If he wants to keep Bill out, he can think about Carrie having her way with him all night.

He's trying to get in again, Trent tells us.

No shit.

Whatever Us-in-Bill's telepathic ability, it likely works best on hospital patients already insensate on drugs, their consciousnesses too wounded to put up much of a fight.

The whispering pauses—and then Bill and the

patients try again, only this time it's one message, one vision, hijacked and remixed: Carrie's body pale in the moonlight, bouncy-bouncy-bouncy, only instead of her delicate face oh God now it's Bill's massive grayflesh head on her sweeping neck, Bill's thick tongue poking from beneath chapped lips, his dry hair whisking up and down, and Bill is grunting louder and louder—

JESUS, Trent screams, his concentration breaking, and the buzzing surges forward, penetrating deep into the brain like a Mongol horde slamming through a fallen gate into a city. But never fear, because we have this, we can deploy our own immense powers to block Bill's assault—

But should you?

That's not Trent's inner voice—it's Us-in-Bill, a psychic megaphone that booms all the way to our toes.

Leave us alone, we tell him. *Just let us do our thing.*

No. We must all be one big happy family. Maximum control. Maximum Freedom.

Trent deserves his own control.

Human beings had their chance. They lost.

Trent screeches for mercy. We pump a dose of adrenaline into his bloodstream—his heart skips a beat—and then follow it up with a memory of the drugs snowing on us in the car wreck, a blinding flare so intense it drives the buzzing back. Just like that, the invasion stops. Trent falls to one knee before we can stop him.

Bill frowns, disappointed. "Watch this," he says, swiping a finger at the patients.

The crowd takes three big steps back, canes and

walkers scraping the tile. Takes a collective breath that sounds like the tide rushing in. Knees popping, gowns flopping open, IV lines whisking the air.

And then they charge the windows.

The first ones smack against the thick glass, which cracks but doesn't break. Then the ones behind them add their weight, flesh flopping against flesh, and the windows pop from their frames in a bright waterfall of shards, and the bodies tumble into the dusk, spiraling and flailing fifty feet to the pavement.

Trent tries to turn away, but we squeeze and pull the tendons in his legs and neck, walking him forward. He screams at us inside his head, calls us all kinds of names, but we need to bear witness to whatever is happening below. In some way, we're responsible for this, so we must see. Why couldn't these people have fought back against Bill, like that one Russian? Why did they have to be so weak?

When the bodies hit, they crumple and explode and leak, until a pile of them lie between the hospital entrance and the rows of SWAT officers. More patients scramble to the windows and leap out, and when they land, they're cushioned by dying flesh. They roll off, and rise to their knees, then to their feet, and hobble forward. Some of the cops and hazmat workers retreat, hollering and screaming, while the more heroic ones press forward, pushing collapsible stretchers, ready to do whatever they can to help.

The stronger patients, bleeding and broken, grapple with that first line of emergency workers, some of whom try to pull back when they realize something's wrong. An old lady, dragging her left leg broken in two places, grips a much larger SWAT cop by his body armor and levers her mouth beneath his helmet, as if going for an awkward kiss. The cop places his hands on her frail shoulders, to shove her away, but he's already taken over. His arms fall away from her and his body spasms, head twisted to the sky.

The rest of the cops and medics fall back too late. We can watch the takeover as it ripples through the crowds around the vans and ambulances, a physical wave.

Welcome to the future.

Bill's hand closes around the back of Trent's neck, squeezes. A low squeal of fear escapes Trent's lips, and his knees tremble. This close, Bill smells meaty, like a chunk of raw beef left in the sun. Before we can react, we feel a prickling at the base of Trent's skull—

20.

W**E'RE BACK ON** the gray beach, the water lapping at our tendrils. Trent stands beside us in the surf, naked except for his leopard-print jacket, shivering in the cold wind slicing down the coast.

"Great." Trent says. "Not this again."

Footsteps crunch sand. Bill strides for us, also naked as the day he was born. A thick mass of tendrils dangles from between his legs, dragging on the sand, yellowish and segmented; when it touches a wetter patch of sand, it crackles and sparks with electricity. Smaller coils wave from his ears and the corner of his left eye-socket. His eyes are black with dried blood, making him look more like a bloated carcass than ever.

"No more negotiations. No more of this useless equivocating. Here's the deal," Bill says. "We're plugged into your brainstem and your cortex."

"Just leave us alone." Trent scoops up a handful of wet gray sand and throws it at his uncle. "Please. I just want to be left alone."

Bill ignores him. He walks up to us, places a hand on our main trunk of tendrils. We try to draw back, only to find ourselves rooted to the spot. Through his touch, a tingling spreads through our cells, warm and syrupy, so overwhelming it threatens to dissolve us into quivering bits. It reminds us of the drugs, or love, but even purer, better. "That's what it feels like," he tells us. "The sensations of a million people, flowing through you. There's nothing you won't experience. This is what we wanted from the beginning, remember? Even love isn't this good. Love doesn't last. This does."

He withdraws his hand, and the sensation disappears, leaving a black void, unbearable. Tears would spring to my eyes, if we could cry, and we resist telling him to touch us again. Instead, we turn to Trent. Even at this worst moment, we want his opinion. We've grown very attached, more than we ever were with Bill. "You get a say in this."

"And I say I want no part of it," Trent shoots back. "You're guests in *my* body."

"Kid, we'll make you a deal," Bill says to him. "In all of your travels today, did you see anything worth preserving? Or was it all just horrible stupidity all the way down?"

Trent turns to the endless ocean, and in the humid shimmering above its surface, we see a blur of color coalesce into shape: Carrie in her ironic shirt, offering us her best screw-you grin. "There's love," he says. "Pure love."

"Your ex," Bill says. "Who delivers drugs. And who ran."

A tear rolls down Trent's cheek. "I know where this is going."

"Trent—" We raise a tendril, beseeching.

"I want to thank you." Trent tells us, his voice rising and rising. "You know what I have to thank you for? When I woke up this morning, I really was feeling like a coward. I really was feeling lost. But now, after everything that we've been through today? That *I've* been through? Now I feel like I have the big ol' hairy balls to say one thing: *Screw you, friend.*"

With that, he sprints away, disappearing into the mist.

"Given time, he might get over it," Bill says. "But it's up to you whether you want him to actually stick around. If not . . . " He pinches two fingers together, as if squishing a small insect. "Easy enough to clear out his consciousness."

"We want him to live."

"Works for me." Bill smiles, and beneath the rumbling of the waves we hear the sounds of the outside world: the crackle of fire and the warbling of sirens, mixed with the screams of people. There are difficult days ahead, but now we understand everything that Us-in-Bill has told us. The events of today have shown us that the human race is fucked beyond repair, no matter what we might have tried to believe. There was never any path besides this one; no route forward that didn't end in our domination. This was best for everyone.

We ask: "Where do we begin?"

"What do you think that body wants first? Cocaine or hamburgers?" Bill claps his hands with glee, his crotch-tendrils spewing bright sparks across the gray sand. "The absolute unit, it has to stay nourished in all ways."

21.

E CAN SENSE Trent deep in the basement of his own mind. He's built a room down there, with a door impossible for us to unlock, but we can peer through the keyhole. The walls are covered with posters of David Bowie and Marilyn Monroe (always a fan of vintage, dear Trent), and a torn leather couch dominates the floor, facing a widescreen television that plays clips from classic films, music videos, memories of Carrie kissing him all over in that wintery bed. By sifting through the abandoned files in Trent's hippocampus, we determine this is a replica of his basement at home, his safe space from life's chaos.

For what it's worth, we whisper through the keyhole, *we're sorry about this.*

Screw off, Trent says, his eyes never leaving the television.

We promise you can come out. You won't be deleted.

Yeah, right. I told you to screw off.

We leave him down there. If he's unwilling to cooperate, his fortress can serve as a prison. Let him watch through the keyhole as we take his body on new adventures. And just wait until we find Carrie, who's aggravatingly managed to dodge our growing network so far—what a grand time we'll all have!

Yes, our future spreads before us, bright and pure. We have more minds to weave into us, more food and drugs to consume, more death-defying stunts to pull with our endless supply of bodies. Our one regret is a small one: that we didn't realize our potential from the very beginning, when we were a cluster of cells in a water glass, on the verge of sliding down Bill's throat and into his welcoming gut.

Why control a single mind when you can control the whole world?

EDIBLE, adj. Good to eat, and wholesome to digest, as a worm to a toad, a toad to a snake, a snake to a pig, a pig to a man, and a man to a worm.

—Ambrose Bierce, "The Devil's Dictionary"

THE END?

Not if you want to dive into more of Crystal Lake Publishing's Tales from the Darkest Depths!

Check out our amazing website and online store (https://www.crystallakepub.com)

We always have great new projects and content on the website to dive into, as well as a newsletter, behind the scenes options, social media platforms, and our own dark fiction shared-world series and our very own store. If you use the IGotMyCLPBook! coupon code in the store (at the checkout), you'll get a one-time-only 50% discount on your first eBook purchase!

Our webstore even has categories specifically for KU books, non-fiction, anthologies, and of course more novels and novellas.

ABOUT THE AUTHOR

Nick Kolakowski is the author of "Boise Longpig Hunting Club," "Love & Bullets," and other grim delights of horror and crime fiction. He also co-edited the Anthony-nominated anthology "Lockdown" with Steve Weddle. He lives and works in New York City.

Readers . . .

It makes our day to know you reached the end of our book. Thank you so much. This is why we do what we do every single day.

Whether you found the book good or great, we'd love to hear what you thought. Please take a moment to leave a short review on Amazon, Goodreads, etc. No need to write an in-depth discussion. Even a single sentence will be greatly appreciated. Reviews go a long way to helping a book sell, and is great for an author's career. It'll also help us to continue publishing quality books. You can also share a photo of yourself holding this book with the hashtag #IGotMyCLPBook!

Thank you again for taking the time to journey with Crystal Lake Publishing.

We are also on . . .

Our Website:
www.crystallakepub.com

Twitter:
https://twitter.com/crystallakepub

Facebook:
https://www.facebook.com/Crystallakepublishing/

Instagram:
https://www.instagram.com/crystal_lake_publishing/

and Patreon:
https://www.patreon.com/CLP

We even have an Amazon page:
amazon.com/author/crystalpublishing

<h2 style="text-align:center">Our Mission Statement:</h2>

Since its founding in August 2012, Crystal Lake Publishing has quickly become one of the world's leading publishers of Dark Fiction and Horror books in print, eBook, and audio formats.

While we strive to present only the highest quality fiction and entertainment, we also endeavour to support authors along their writing journey. We offer our time and experience in non-fiction projects, as well as author mentoring and services, at competitive prices.

With several Bram Stoker Award wins and many other wins and nominations (including the HWA's Specialty Press Award), Crystal Lake Publishing puts integrity, honor, and respect at the forefront of our publishing operations.

We strive for each book and outreach program we spearhead to not only entertain and touch or comment on issues that affect our readers, but also to strengthen and support the Dark Fiction field and its authors.

Not only do we find and publish authors we believe are destined for greatness, but we strive to work with men and woman who endeavour to be decent human beings who care more for others than themselves, while still being hard working, driven, and passionate artists and storytellers.

Crystal Lake Publishing is and will always be a beacon of what passion and dedication, combined with overwhelming teamwork and respect, can accomplish. We endeavour to know each and every one of our readers, while building personal relationships with our authors, reviewers, bloggers, podcasters, bookstores, and libraries.

We will be as trustworthy, forthright, and

transparent as any business can be, while also keeping most of the headaches away from our authors, since it's our job to solve the problems so they can stay in a creative mind. Which of course also means paying our authors.

We do not just publish books, we present to you worlds within your world, doors within your mind, from talented authors who sacrifice so much for a moment of your time.

There are some amazing small presses out there, and through collaboration and open forums we will continue to support other presses in the goal of helping authors and showing the world what quality small presses are capable of accomplishing. No one wins when a small press goes down, so we will always be there to support hardworking, legitimate presses and their authors. We don't see Crystal Lake as the best press out there, but we will always strive to be the best, strive to be the most interactive and grateful, and even blessed press around. No matter what happens over time, we will also take our mission very seriously while appreciating where we are and enjoying the journey.

What do we offer our authors that they can't do for themselves through self-publishing?

We are big supporters of self-publishing (especially hybrid publishing), if done with care, patience, and planning. However, not every author has the time or inclination to do market research, advertise, and set up book launch strategies. Although a lot of authors are successful in doing it all, strong small presses will always be there for the authors who just want to do what they do best: write.

What we offer is experience, industry knowledge, contacts and trust built up over years. And due to our strong brand and trusting fanbase, every Crystal Lake

Publishing book comes with weight of respect. In time our fans begin to trust our judgment and will try a new author purely based on our support of said author.

With each launch we strive to fine-tune our approach, learn from our mistakes, and increase our reach. We continue to assure our authors that we're here for them and that we'll carry the weight of the launch and dealing with third parties while they focus on their strengths—be it writing, interviews, blogs, signings, etc.

We also offer several mentoring packages to authors that include knowledge and skills they can use in both traditional and self-publishing endeavours.

We look forward to launching many new careers.

This is what we believe in. What we stand for. This will be our legacy.

**Welcome to Crystal Lake Publishing—
Tales from the Darkest Depths.**